The
Golden
Strand

By Gregory T. Glading

Table of Contents

Chapter 1 1

Chapter 2 10

Chapter 3 17

Chapter 4 22

Chapter 5 30

Chapter 6 37

Chapter 7 41

Chapter 8 46

Chapter 9 60

Chapter 10 64

Chapter 11 67

Part II 81

Chapter 1 83

Chapter 2 99

Chapter 3 104

Chapter 4 110

Chapter 5 121

Chapter 6 129

Chapter 7 139

Chapter 8 142

Chapter 9 148

Chapter 10 153

Chapter 11 157

Chapter 12 163

Chapter 13 173

Chapter 14 179

Chapter 15 184

Chapter 16 192

Chapter 17 199

Chapter 18 204

Chapter 19 210

Chapter 20 215

Chapter 21 218

Chapter 22 231

Chapter 23 233

Chapter 24 238

Chapter 25 240

Chapter 26 242

Epilogue 250

Chapter 1

Spence Carter planted his ten-foot-long Hobie surfboard upright in the sand. He rubbed its fiberglass crinkles and gazed over the Pacific. The setting Sun inched closer to the horizon like an opening treasure chest, spilling its gold across the sea. Warm saltwater washed over his feet, luring him to take one last ride. He leaped into the ocean with his surfboard, smiling as salt water splashed his face. He paddled to a strategic spot beyond the break. *'Neptune, Poseidon, Gaia, whoever is in charge of the sea,'* he cupped his hand, scooped up ocean water, and sprinkled it on his head, *'send me a big one.'* A large swell rolled in from the distance. "Thank you!" He paddled furiously, racing the ocean as the swell rose and steepened. His board slid down the face. He stood. Wind and salty spray buffeted him. The ocean roared. Speeding into the wave's pocket, he raised his hands to enhance his balance.

"Look out, buddy! Coming through!" another surfer shouted as he sped below in the trough. Spence shifted up to the wave's lip to avoid him. He performed a snap maneuver, using his back foot to apply pressure for a sharp, controlled pivot, and re-entered the curl.

The surfer forced two others to kick out. "Woo!" He yelled as he shifted to the nose of the board and *'hanged ten.'* He raised his arms. "I'm the king of the ocean, baby!"

Spence shook his head and smirked, *'He's at it again,'* as he rode the wave to its shoulder and let the white water take him to shore.

***

Spence jammed his surfboard into the sand with others. The surfboards resembled a fiberglass Stonehenge. A dozen male surfers, three female surfers, and seven local gals had gathered around a campfire. The nearby Santa Monica Pier added lighting. A full moon glowed in the eastern sky. A *Zenith Royal 1000* transistor radio played Jan and Dean's *Drag City.'* A pink bikini-clad woman in her early twenties with a body honed from volleyball and surfing trotted over and embraced Spence. Muscular without steroids, his six-foot-three height stood half a foot above her. "Spence. I'm so glad you're not working tonight." She beamed. "So, let's dance."

Spence wrapped his arm around her firm waist. "Sure, Penny, but are you down for my fight at the Huntington Beach Auditorium tomorrow night?" He stroked her hair. Its tint matched her white pearl necklace, passed down from her grandmother to her mother. "I'd appreciate it."

"You know I don't like professional wrestling." She grabbed a handful of his golden blonde hair. "I love you despite it, not because of it." She laughed and pulled on his hair. "Besides, it's fake, unlike this," she planted a wet kiss on his lips. "But, hey, just for you, I'll go. And how about afterward you take me to the Coconut Club? The Rip Chords are performing." She tilted her head back and touched her chin to his.

"Deal." He kissed her.

Penny moved her face back, put her hands on his shoulders, and smiled. "Do you know what time you're wrestling? I hope you won't mind my arriving a little before you're on, and if we leave early, so we won't miss a set of The Rip Chords?"

"I wrestle second to last, around ten PM. I'll shower and change right away. If we move fast, we can beat the traffic." Spence put his arms around her and kissed her lips. "Let me get you a cup of beer from the keg. Let's enjoy the evening. It's gotta be a short one, however. You know, tomorrow it's up with the sun to work out with Rick and get in a session with the waves before preparing for the show."

Penny placed her left hand on his pectorals and tapped his lips with her right forefinger. "You know what they say about all work and no play."

"Some would call working out, surfing, and wrestling play. Nevertheless, it pays." He grinned. "It supports two other hobbies." He grinned. "Eating and sleeping indoors."

She chuckled, "I know someday I'll come first with you. Until then, I figure I gotta take what I can get." She planted another wet kiss on his lips. "I do appreciate your seriousness, unlike your pal." She pointed at Sonny Dyer toting his surfboard and running toward them.

"Now the party begins!" Sonny Dyer stood three inches shorter than Spence and had a body toned from swimming rather than weightlifting. The Sun turned his skin lobster red and his hair a lighter shade of dark brown. A smile enhanced his handsome, oval face as he stuck his surfboard into the sand. "I'm here! I'm more than the King of the Ocean- I'm the Ocean's king! Now behold." He beat his chest like a gorilla. "The ultimate party animal."

The two surfers he bumped from their waves confronted him. A lean surfer with short, curly brown hair shoved Sonny's chest. "You may think you're hot stuff for winning the Malibu International, but it doesn't give you a free pass to kick us off our wave."

"Hey, Scott. It's like, you can't stand the heat, get out of the ocean."

Scott stepped up, hooked his foot behind Sonny's ankle, and shoved him onto the ground. "I don't think you get it, Sonny boy. We're going to give you a lesson in surfing etiquette." He kicked sand in Sonny's face.

"Two against one." Sonny wiped away the sand. "I'm impressed, dudes."

"Consider it the school of hard knocks." Scott kicked his leg. "Now, get up and take your medicine." He raised his fists.

"Hey! Hey!" Spence grabbed his arm. "Come on, Scott. There's no need for that. This is a beach party. Ya want a battle royale? Be at the Huntington Beach Auditorium tomorrow night. We can use the ring after the show."

"All right, Spence." Scott lowered his fist. "How about you teach your friend the easy way? You won't always be here to stop him from learning the hard way.

Scott and his friend left and rejoined the party. Spence extended his arm and helped Sonny to his feet. "I don't know why I'm buddies with you. I guess it's because I never had a little brother to keep out of trouble."

"Well, thanks, bro." Sonny dusted the sand from his body. "I could've taken any one of 'em. Only you can win two against one."

"Look, Sonny, you're the best surfer here. Everyone knows it. After all, you have the trophies and sponsorships to prove it. Yeah, we all know the unwritten rule. The better surfer gets priority on a wave. Still, you gotta cut the monkey business." Spence put his hand on Sonny's shoulder. "Not just because I won't always be around to bail your ass outta trouble, but, damn Sonny, how about thinking of someone besides yourself for once."

"When I get my big break in acting, I'll make it all up to you." Sonny beamed, "Every one of you." The transistor radio played The Beach Boys *'Dance, Dance, Dance'*. Right now, I'm not in a thinking mood. I'm up for some dancing. The king of the waves is also king of the dance floor." Sonny walked over, grabbed the hand of one of three girls standing together, and pulled her to the dance area. She grimaced. After perusing his face, she smiled. Thirty seconds later, they danced in rhythm and synch.

Spence put his hands on his hips and shook his head. Penny came over and took his hand. "What are you waiting for?" Spence and Penny joined the others in dance.

***

Penny pointed to Sonny and the trim brunette with an inward curl that he had danced with all evening. "It looks like your buddy is in love."

"You don't know Sonny like I do." Spence shook his head. "She better guard her heart like the crown jewels."

"Judging by how they're kissing." Penny giggled. "I think he already stole the crown jewels and snuck out of the palace." The transistor radio played the Beach Boys *'Surfer Girl.'* "How about one last dance before you take me home?" Spence and Penny slow danced and kissed.

***

Spence smothered his wind-up alarm clock with his pillow. *'Five am.'* He moved as slowly and stealthily as possible.

5

Penny stirred. She half opened her eyes and grasped his hand. "Please stay. Come on." Penny tugged him toward her. "Stay with me."

"I'd love to stay, Penny," Spence yanked his arm away. "Rick is waiting for me. Working out is part of my bread and butter." He smiled.

"So, working out with Rick is better than making love to me." She reached for his arm. "Come back to bed."

Spence pulled his arm back. "Hey? How about I pick you up for lunch? We can hang out on the beach a bit before the matches."

"You won't be hanging out with me." She sat up. "You'll be catching some waves while I sit and watch. I'd better study and finish my designs for the fashion show." She rubbed her eyes. "I'll catch you around ten after your show." Penny scrunched onto her side and went back to sleep.

***

"Hey, you're five minutes late." Rick Drasich met Spence at the gym door. The place was less gym and more dungeon. No windows held in its dank odor. Floor fans provided the only ventilation and a bare overhead light bulb its only lighting. Clanging weights sounded like dinner plates in a busy restaurant. Curly blond hair topped Rick's angular face, strong jawline, and pointed chin. Like Spence, he had a solid, proportional physique. "Hurry up and spot me. While you were lollygagging, I worked up to three forty-fives on each side. We're going to hit four hundred today."

Rick lay on his back and gripped the cambered bar. Spence stood behind him and lifted the bar from the upright. Rick knocked out ten reps before Spence guided the bar back to the uprights. Rick sat up, "I hope you can get to the

Coconut Club in time to see my band, *The Epics.* We open for the Rip Chords.

"Come on, Rick, you're better than an opening act. Besides, what are they paying you for a set? You're a fine bass player, but a name earned elsewhere will help you rise above the crowd. Let me help get you into wrestling. You got the look and physique. We've surfed together. I can tell you're an athlete. What do you say?"

"I'm intrigued." Rick stood and walked behind the bar. "I've told you that before. But what better day job than a beach lifeguard? Where else can I make a living looking at chicks and working on a tan?"

"You can wrestle part-time. Besides, most of our gigs are at night. Let's start by practicing some falls on the beach after our workout. Come to the matches with me tonight. I'll introduce you to my promoter and some of the boys." Spence lay under the bar and gripped it.

"That's three-fifteen." Rick put his hands on his hips. "You're not going to warm up first?"

"What's the matter? You don't like me catching up to you too quickly?"

Rick stood behind the bar and grasped it.

"Not so fast. I don't need a lift-off. What you can do is turn up the radio. That's a good song. The radio played, The Flee-Rekkers *Sunday Date.*"

"I'll do you one better. You and Penny show up at the Coconut Club before my set, and we'll play that for you."

Spence knocked off ten reps before returning the bar to the rack.

"Not bad, bro. You're gettin' a pump already. I see Penny's got you inspired to look even better. She's one hot babe. You better not let her go."

Spence sat up. "Five years ago, as you know, I was one half of the American Federation of Wrestling tag-team championship playing an ornery cowboy named Biff Rustler. I haven't even gotten a minor title with the Western Wrestling Alliance. If I want to advance my career, I'll have to move on. I don't know if I can give up the California sun and surf. Moreover, Penny is a true California girl, and she's in fashion design school. I can't ask her to join me elsewhere. What looked like a great future four years ago now looks uncertain."

The radio played The Shadows, *Wonderful Land.*

"A true California gal she is." Rick grinned. "I have no doubt the Beach Boys used her as their inspiration for *California Girls.* Besides, Penny loves you." Rick leaned on the bar. "And I think she understands where you're at."

"I know that." Spence wiped the sweat from his brow. "But is it fair to her? She could get a multi-millionaire if she wanted."

"That's exactly why you don't want to lose her. She's not into big bucks. She's into you. Open your eyes, man. Don't be a fool."

"I know you're right, but I wanna be more settled. I've lost my vision for the future." Spence grabbed two twenty-five-pound plates. He handed one to Rick. "Let's go for three-sixty-five before we hit four hundred."

***

8

Spence and Rick carried their surfboards onto the beach. Sonny, also toting his surfboard, ran up to them. "Uh oh, look at you two," he pointed at them, "now they gotta rename this place Muscle Beach. I hope you two aren't too stiff to paddle out with me. Better yet. Wait on shore." Sonny pointed to a portable radio playing Jan and Dean's *Ride The Wild Surf.* "I would hardly call those waves wild surf. They're a bit on the small side and breaking close to shore. As soon as I start hotdogging it up, I'll have everyone on the beach, meaning more people watching me surf than see you wrestle," Sonny pointed at Spence, "Or listen to the Epics." He pointed at Rick.

Spence and Rick stood with their hands on their hips as Sonny ran ahead to the ocean. Several people on the beach recognized Sonny. They stood in ankle-deep water and waited to see Sonny's first ride. He caught a wave, got into the pocket, and walked up and down the board. He then performed a handstand. Some of the onlookers clapped and cheered.

"You gotta admit." Spence turned to Ric. "He is good."

"Yeah." Rick kept his hands on his hips. "Too bad he knows it."

"I also know that you can play bass guitar. But I still haven't taught you how to fall." Spence put his ankle behind Rick and tripped him backward.

Rick flopped onto his back.

"You call that a fall?" Spence laughed. "You fell like a sack of potatoes."

"You son-of-a-gun." Rick sat up, bracing himself on his elbows. "One of these days." He smiled and shook his head. "One of these days."

Chapter 2

Spence entered the Huntington Beach Auditorium dressing room and put his kitbag onto a bench. Western Wrestling Alliance promoter Simon Beck walked up to him. He placed his briefcase on the bench and adjusted his wire-framed, half-eye glasses on his long, skinny nose. "Tonight, I'm letting you go over with Spider. You have the greater following here. You'll do the same match when we work the Sacramento area, except when he applies the claw hold, you submit instead of escaping. Central California is his neck of the woods. You worked together in Florida. I like how you two work here."

"In Florida, we were both heels and rarely wrestled each other. So, what other favors do you have to offer?"

"I gave you a chance to go back to Florida with Al Cohen or take Stan Hartman's offer in Chicago." Simon straightened his narrow shoulders and concave chest. "You renewed your contract with me. You want to work in California? You do what I want. You only have fifteen matches left on your deal. Until then, don't question me or complain."

"Come on, Simon. Back in Florida, I was half of the World Tag Team championship. I was the main event in the biggest show in the history of the business."

"Your opponents were the main event. My territory doesn't need a Biff Rustler. 1963 is not 1958, and California is not Florida. Moreover, I can pick and choose from any number of well-built beach boys. I can replace you tomorrow, and as far as I'm concerned, you're overpaid."

Simon prodded. "Don't you forget it. Now, I expect a good match with Spider."

***

Ding. Ding, Ding. After the bell, the ring announcer held a large microphone up to his lips. "Ladies and Gentlemen. In the red corner, hailing from Johannesburg, South Africa, he stands 6-8 inches tall and weighs 220 pounds. Spider Nel.

The crowd booed as Spider Nel gripped his right wrist with his left hand and brandished his long, black-painted fingernails like a claw. He wore black tights with straps over his shoulders. Spider webs were tattooed on his arms, deltoids, and neck. He had dyed his hair ink-black and applied copious black eye shadow.

"In the blue corner, everybody's favorite, from the beaches of Southern California, The Golden Surfer, Spence Carter." Spence raised and shook his fists to audience applause.

Five minutes into the match, Spence had Spider in a headlock. He scanned the audience, looking for Penny. He found her sitting in the fourth row from the ring. Her blank expression showed disinterest. They made eye contact. She smiled and waved. Spence smiled back. Spider then broke the hold by pushing Spence into the ropes. He clotheslined him on the rebound and then stomped on him. With each right foot stomp on Spence's body, Spider stomped his left foot on the mat for a sound effect. Spence climbed to one knee and started clapping his hands. The audience clapped with him. He reached his feet and hurled Spider into the ropes. He drop-kicked Spider on the rebound and put him in an armbar. Spence held the arm bar as he lifted him and spun him. Spider eye-gouged him, breaking the hold. He then put

11

his clawed hand over Spence's face. Spence thrashed in pain, waving his arms wildly.

The referee leaned to Spence and asked loudly, articulating his lips for the audience to read, "Do you submit?"

"No! No!" He continued waving his arms. He staggered to the ring's edge and grabbed the top rope. The referee forced Spider to break the hold. Spence then flung Spider into the ropes. Spider rebounded. Spence leaped over him, grabbed his ankles on the descent, and rolled Spider onto his back. Spence secured his shoulders with his legs. The referee slapped the mat, "One. Two. Three." He raised Spence's hand in victory. The crowd stood and cheered. Spence spotted Penny. She remained seated, smiling without clapping.

***

After showering, Spence grabbed his kitbag and hastily left the locker room. Penny greeted him with a kiss. She pulled him by the hand. "Let's go. I know you want to catch Rick's set."

"I do, too. Moreover, I want to avoid Beck. The less I see of him, the better." Spence pulled away from her. "Just let me stick my head in the other dressing room and say a quick goodbye to Spider. We had a good match, and he sold my moves to the audience." Spence winked at Penny. "I have to return the favor next week in Sacramento."

Spence and Penny left before the autograph seekers gathered at the exit. The cheering and booing for the main event cloaked their conversation. They walked hand in hand to his '62 red Chevrolet Impala SS Convertible. The top was down. He tossed his kitbag into the back seat and opened the passenger door for Penny, circled the car, vaulted over the door, cranked the ignition, and revved its V8 409 engine. "I put a four-barrel carburetor and headers on her. I wish the wrestling fans roared for me like that." He turned and grinned. "Now let's test 'er." He floored the accelerator. The G-force thrust Penny back in her seat. Screeching tires and the scent of burning rubber were the exclamation mark. They pulled out of the parking lot and sped down the main road. Spence glanced to his right and smiled as the wind blew Penny's long blond hair back like streamers. Penny returned his smile. Spence turned up the volume of the radio. It played the Jive Fives', *The Girl with the Wind in Her Hair.*

***

The Coconut Club's doorman recognized Spence and Penny, waived the cover charge, and passed them in. The Coconut Club had four plastic coconut trees in a vain attempt to create a tropical aura. Tonight, the packed house created its vibe. The crowd allowed Spence and Penny to weave their way toward the stage. One young man murmured to his female companion, "Hey, that's Spence Carter, the Golden Surfer."

Another young man grabbed his male friend's arm and pointed at Penny, "Check out that blonde."

"She's a knockout, all right. But judging by the size of her boyfriend, he can knock us out if we try anything."

"Hey! Spence! Penny!" Sonny Dyer had a lovely, richly tanned Mexican girl on his arm. She wore a green and red dress with a red swath around her trim waist. The ends of her short sleeves were ruffled. "Imagine," Sonny chuckled. "You fight to the finish with Spider Nel yet show up fresh as a daisy, without a mark on you." Sonny leaned toward his date.

13

"Juanita, these are my friends. He's professional wrestler Spence Carter, the Golden Surfer. You must think the world-class beauty on his arm is the reigning Miss Universe, but it's my friend, Penny Williams." Sonny reached out and held Penny's hand. "Spence, Penny, this is Juanita."

Juanita smiled shyly. She extended a limp wristed hand to Spence and Penny. Both gently touched her hand.

"Hey, I got some big news." Sonny put his arm around Juanita. "My agent got me an audition tomorrow with United International Pictures. It's one of those beach party movies. My agent says getting the part is a sure thing. I just gotta play myself. Moreover, he says they want my name in the credits because I won the Malibu International. They want a scene of me surfing." Sonny clasped Spence's shoulder. "Hey, bro, I'll put in a word for you. I'm sure they'll need extras."

"That's wonderful!" Penny smiled. "I hope it proves your big break."

"Me too!" Sonny beamed. "And Penny, I'll put money on it that you're prettier by a mile than anyone on the set." Sonny laughed. "If your boyfriend here couldn't beat the daylights out of me, I could never resist that smile. I know no casting director can."

"I have no acting talent." Penny chuckled. "I think I'll stick to fashion design." Penny smiled at Spence. "If Simon Legree, I mean, Simon Beck, will let you go, I think you should give it a try."

"Let's first wait and see if Sonny can actually get me an audition." Spence put his arm around Penny. "We'll talk about it then. I only have fifteen matches left in my wrestling contract. We'll take it from there."

"Come on, Spence," Sonny sipped his beer. "Opportunity only knocks once. When it does, you better answer the door."

The house lights suddenly dimmed. A spotlight shone on the master of ceremonies. He wore sandals, flower-patterned swim shorts, a Hawaiian *lei* around his neck, and a tropical print shirt. "Tonight, our feature band is the Rip Chords. Our opening act surely won't disappoint. Ladies and Gentlemen. The Coconut Club proudly presents the Epics."

The four members of the Epics took the stage. Rick Drasich winked at Spence and Penny. His band opened with the instrumental *"Sunday Date."*

***

After the Epic's set, Rick joined Spence, Penny, Sonny, and Juanita.

"You played wonderfully." Penny smiled. "I know someday you guys will get your big break."

"And you kept your promise to play, *Sunday Date.* You sure play a mean bass, and your lead guitarist played *Apache* like The Shadows' Hank Marvin."

I'll go get him. I know he'd like to hear it from you." Rick chuckled. "Every guitarist in the business wants to be compared to Hank Marvin."

"Hank Marvin is an Englishman, and his skinny body and thick black glasses make him look, as they say across the other ocean, *boffin.* Look at you, though." Sonny pointed at Rick. "You've got a great physique and, if you look up Californian in the dictionary, we'll find your picture.

"I'll be the first to admit. The Epics aren't The Ventures or The Shadows. Spence, I want to take you up on your offer.

Introduce me to your promoter. I don't want to give up my beach patrol gig just yet. Nevertheless, getting some notoriety as a wrestler might give me my edge as a musician."

"I work tomorrow night in San Diego. Why don't you ride along with me? I'll recommend you to the promoter. Professional wrestling is not as easy as it looks. Yet you have all the essentials for success in the business. I'm sure some of the boys will happily teach you the tricks of the trade."

"As for me," Sonny pointed to himself. I must be at the studio at six am tomorrow morning.

Penny tilted her head. "Shouldn't you get some sleep?"

"I'll get plenty of sleep when I'm dead."

Juanita laughed. "Ay Dios mio." She wrapped her arm around Sonny.

Chapter 3

Sonny drove his yellow Deuce Coupe to the security gate of United International Pictures. The guard checked his credentials, gave him a parking pass, and waved him in. After parking in the cast and crew lot, he perused his scrawl on scrap paper. *'Stage 7. Where is the Hollywood glamour? These buildings look like warehouses.'*

After a fifteen-minute walk, Sonny found Stage 7. Inside were over a hundred young men and women in beach attire. Some were reciting lines aloud; others were singing a cappella. Sonny scanned the room. A woman with wavy brunette hair cascading below her shoulders made eye contact with him. She wore an Oxford blue, knee-length linen skirt, a white silk blouse, and a matching Oxford blue collared jacket.

'Oh my God!' Sonny gasped; his eyes opened wide. 'She's gorgeous. I've dated the West Coast's hottest beach babes and party gals. Never anyone like her.' He pinched his chin. 'Even her perfectly toned arms and how gracefully she raises her clipboard." Sonny stood still as she approached him.

"Sonny Dyer." She extended her hand. "I'm Sammi Wray, associate producer of Beach Party USA."

Sonny shook her hand. 'Firm but gentle. I don't want to let go.' He imbibed her hyacinth aroma. 'Her skin is like porcelain, framing perfect cheekbones. Get a grip, Sonny. Don't let her exotic brown eyes and those fluttering black eyelashes make you act stupid.'

"Follow me. I want to introduce you to Mr. Feldman, the producer." Her hair swished as she turned her head to direct Sonny.

Arthur Feldman sat behind his oak desk with his palms down on the desktop. The short and stout producer had a wide forehead with dark hair siding his bald pate. A visible vein ran down his right temple. "Sonny Dyer. Your agent sent you here to audition for the role of a surfer in my star, Johnny Bright's, clique. I already know everything I need to know about you. This interview is less an audition and more me ensuring you understand what I expect." The producer's palms remained on the table. He nudged his head forward and focused on Sonny. "You will do as I say, as Miss Wray says, and what my director, his assistants, or anyone else in my production staff says, and you will do so without hesitation or question. Am I understood?"

Sonny slumped his shoulders. "Yes, sir."

"This movie is not *Gone with the Wind* or *The Ten Commandments*. It's not a Bruce Brown documentary, either. Call it vapid all you want. I am not making Beach Party USA for surfers, Californians, or Floridians. My movies relieve people living in places like New York, Philadelphia, and Detroit from the drudgery of a cold, gray Winter. A ticket to my movie is a hell of a lot cheaper than an airline ticket to a tropical beach. That's my business model, and thus far, it's made our investors gobs of money. Therefore, we must finish shooting by the end of summer and have it ready for release right after the holidays. We will shoot some scenes on the beach. Unfortunately, I can't order around Mother Nature like I do the plebes who take my paychecks. Much of the filming will take place right here on stage 7. "Never forget," Arthur Feldman prodded at Sonny, "I can make you or break you. We will use footage of you winning the Malibu International. I will have a scene of you hotdogging on small waves. My connections report to me on surfing conditions. When the waves are right, someone on my staff will call you. Fail to make yourself available at a second notice, and you're fired and blacklisted from ever making another movie. Am I understood?"

"Yes. Sir."

"That's good. This movie may prove your big break. I will send the contract to your agent. I suggest you sign it without delay. This is not up for negotiation." Arthur Feldman prodded. "Look at the crowd outside my office. You beach boys and girls are a dime-a-dozen." He returned his palms to the table.

"Arthur, we've got plenty of candidates to be part of Johnny's group." Sammi folded her hands in front of her. "Central casting failed to find anyone formidable looking enough for their rivals, The Scorpions."

Sonny raised his hand like a schoolboy. "Sir, my best friend is Spence Carter, the wrestler, The Golden Surfer; he and his training partner, Rick Drasich, who performs in a rock and roll band called the Epics, would make ideal Scorpions."

Arthur Feldman narrowed his eyes, raised his eyebrows, and tilted his head. "I know of Spence Carter. I remember when he fought the Jaguar and Abede the African Lion on national TV. That was five years ago. He's done little since." He smirked. "We own a minority share of the Western Wrestling Alliance. It's my job to know those things." He touched his fingertips in a steeple. "The Epics are just another bar band. Nevertheless, Rick Drasich does look the part." Arthur Feldman pointed his steepled fingers at Sonny. "There's no potential talent in show business that I am unaware of, and if I don't know about someone, one of my minions finds them. That includes sports, music, and theater. I see Carter has trimmed down lately." Arthur Feldman folded his hands and relaxed. "Okay, Mr. Dyer. Give their contact information to Miss Wray. I may consider them."

"Thanks, Mr. Feldman." Sonny smiled for the first time since the meeting began.

"Don't call us. We'll call you when you're needed. Sammi. Please show Mr. Dyer out."

Sammi led Sonny through the throngs of auditioners to the Stage 7 exit. Sonny looked back and winked at her. Sammi did not return the gesture or even smile. She closed the door behind him.

Sonny sniffed the final molecules of her scent. He closed his eyes. *'Don't go back in.'* He dropped his head. His mind spun electric sparks. He pictured her smiling at him. Light flashed in his mind. *'I'm gonna be a movie star; I'm gonna be famous.'* He picked up his step. *'Just wait 'till I tell Spence and Rick.'*

***

Sonny bolted into the gym. Rick stood in front of Spence. With one finger on the bar, Rick helped Spence finish a final rep of overhead presses. "Hey guys! Do I have news for you! I got Arthur Feldman, the producer of Beach Party USA, to consider using you in the flick."

"How is that?" Spence dropped the weight with a thud and rattle.

"He needs people to play in the rival gang. He needs big, mean-looking dudes."

"I may be big." Rick chuckled. "Nobody thinks I look mean."

"Spence," Sonny pointed at him. "You convinced the entire nation that you were Biff Rustler, a mean, onery cowboy. I bet you can do it again."

Spence and Rick looked at each other and nodded.

"I'm still having trouble convincing this one to be a wrestler." Spence chuckled. "Here you march in and make us movie stars."

"Expect a call." Sonny beamed. 'She'll be impressed with me getting them cast,' he thought.

Chapter 4

Penny sat next to Spence in his '62 Chevy Impala convertible. Sonny and Rick rode in the back seat. They stopped at the United International Pictures security gate. "Sonny Dyer." He held his Identification card to the guard. Sonny and Rick sat in the back seat. The guard looked at them. Both flashed their invitation letters and driver's licenses.

. "How about you?" The guard pointed at Penny.

"She doesn't have her card yet." Sonny smiled at the guard.

"I'm sorry, ma'am." The guard focused on Penny. "I can't let you in without credentials."

"Hey, come on, man." Sonny flashed a smile at the guard. "Her beauty is her credential."

"Look, buddy, every day beautiful women pass through this gate. No credentials? No admittance."

Sonny leaned his arm on the window frame. "You say you've seen lots of beauties." He pointed at Penny. "When last one this beautiful?"

Penny flashed a toothy grin.

The guard glanced at her straight white teeth before staring at her bust.

"You know how strict Mr. Feldman is about time." Sonny grinned. "You want to explain to him why you delayed his movie?

"Okay. Miss." The guard breathed heavier. "Next time, bring your ID." He beamed and winked.

She nodded back.

***

"Wow!" Sonny dropped his jaw. "Last time I was here, this place was an empty warehouse. Now look." Stage 7 was converted into a beach. The entire East wall was a movie screen showing the ocean and waves. Sonny's heart skipped a beat. He spotted Sammi talking to two men wearing executive suits. "She's the associate producer." Sonny pointed at Sammi. "She'll tell us what to do next." Sonny led Spence and Rick over to the associate producer. Sonny stood speechless as Sammi ignored him while talking with the two executives.

"Excuse me." She nodded to the executives. "Sonny Dyer. Good to see you on time. These men are James Levine and Jerry Browning. They are two of our most important investors. I see you brought my new Scorpions."

"Yes." Sonny fixed on Sammi. "Spence Carter and Rick Drasich."

"Thank you, Sonny. Now, please get in costume. Dressing room A is over there." Sammi pointed at a portal with the letter "A" painted above it. She next shouted to a petite, young female with thin hair wearing horn-rimmed glasses. She held a clipboard. "Myrna. These two are cast as members of Zurlein's motorcycle gang. Take them to dressing room C and get them fitted with black slacks and leather vests. And you," Sammi smiled at Penny. "Wow! Central casting failed to find big, mean actors to play motorcycle gangsters, but they went above and beyond in finding a dance partner for Johnny." Sammi looked Penny up and down. "I'm not sure I can use you. I want to make Bernadette Hennesey jealous, not upstage her."

23

"Bernadette Hennesey? She's a star." Penny blushed. "I'm just Penny Williams."

"We have several dancing scenes." Sammi smiled at Penny. "I looked over the extras, hoping to find the right girl to dance with Johnny while the camera focused on Bernadette seething in jealousy. Unfortunately, none are pretty enough to pull it off." She looked into Penny's eyes and smiled. "Can you dance?"

"I'm not a trained dancer." Penny raised her hand. "Just parties and clubs for fun."

"You'll do fine." She put both hands on Penny's shoulders.

"But I'm not an extra." Penny lowered her head. "I'm Spence Carter's girlfriend. I'm only tagging along as his guest."

"His guest?" Sammi took her hands from Penny's shoulders. "This studio is for working cast and crew only. I don't know how you got in." Sammi smiled and looked into Penny's eyes. "But I'm glad you did. Even so," Sammi chuckled. "Casting is my decision. I will also have some words with security about letting unauthorized parties into the studio."

Penny blanched.

"It's okay, honey." Sammi reached out and held Penny's hand. "You can watch for now." Sammi beamed. "What would you say if I offered you the role I just discussed?"

Penny blushed. "I'm flattered. But I'm studying design. I can't just up and leave. Besides, I've never acted."

"Wise choice." Sammi pursed her lips. "This business will use you, abuse you, then discard you like yesterday's garbage." She grinned and regained eye contact. "Unless you have the right people looking after you. For now, stay in school. Design?" Sammi chuckled. "I wonder if the world's top designers can make something worthy of you. When you finish school," Sammi reached into her Hermes handbag and drew a business card, giving it to Penny in one fluid motion, "and put together a portfolio, call me. I may have a position for you designing our costumes." Sammi again looked Penny up and down and sighed. "I've never come close to begging anyone to play a part." Sammi placed her right hand on Penny's left shoulder. "Usually, I wait for them to beg me." Sammi chuckled. "Please. Take my offer. Dancing with Johnny will be your only scene." Sammi smiled. "I promise." She chuckled, "That's my promise, not a Hollywood promise. We should have the shot done in an hour." Sammi suddenly turned and glowered at Sonny. "Do you have a question for me?"

Sonny's lips quivered.

"So, what are you waiting for? Hurry up and get in costume. Mr. Feldman told you every second of delay costs him money, and I have an impatient director."

Sonny's vocal cords froze. He took one last look at her before retreating to the dressing room.

Sammi again focused on Penny. "Sweetheart. Does your boyfriend like baseball?"

"Yes!" Penny smiled. "He loves baseball as much as he loves wrestling, surfing, and fast cars."

"Wait here while I get something from my office." Three minutes later, Sammi returned and held up two tickets like a pair of aces. "Here's two deluxe box seat tickets to the

Dodgers. Take your boyfriend and discuss my offer with him." She winked at Penny.

"Why, thank you." Penny held the tickets to her eyes and smiled.

"No. Thank you." Sammi smiled and fluttered her eyelashes. "That's my bribe to sway your boyfriend to convince you to take my offer. This film will be forgotten like fifty others of its ilk. Nevertheless, having your name on the credits as the girl who made Bernadette Hennesey jealous will look good on any resume."

***

Director Andrew Sparks had a graying stubble of a beard; he wore a tweed jacket and wire-framed glasses low on his nose. "Okay, Dyer, you're on." He crossed his legs at his knees and locked his hands behind his head. "After you yell, 'Surf's Up,' count to two. That's one, two. Then run with your surfboard to the ocean. Johnny will follow. It's that simple. You get one shot. Screw it up, and I'll use Nick." The director looked toward another actor before placing his forearm on his folded right leg. "

The assistant director shouted, "Quiet on the set."

Andrew followed with, "Action."

"Surf's up!" Sonny smiled at the camera. Two seconds later, he ran with his surfboard toward the film image of the ocean. Johnny followed.

"That's a wrap." The director stood. "Dyer, stay by your phone. We'll call you when we do the surfing scene on location."

***

Spence, Penny, Sonny, and Rick sat at a table in the Mako Tavern. Spence picked up their pitcher of Lucky Lager beer. He filled Penny's three-quarter full glass, Rick's half-full glass, and Sonny's empty glass. Sonny sat with his elbow on his knee and chin in his hand.

Sonny pictured Sammi. He imagined her in a loose-fitting, informal sun dress. 'Her lips, so fulsome and mellow.' She sipped Lucky Lager beer from her glass, leaving a lipstick mark on the rim. Sonny then drank from her glass, putting his lips over the mark. He stared into her rich brown, almond-shaped eyes…'

"Sonny!" Spence put the pitcher on the table. "Are you here or not here?'

"It's nothing?"

"Nothing?" Rick sipped his beer. "We usually can't shut you up. Did something go wrong on the set?"

"No. No. Nothing at all." Sonny snapped upright. "My scene went perfectly. They'll call me when it's time to film the surfing scene."

"I was going to wait and discuss this with you later," Penny turned to Spence. "Sammi Wray, the associate producer, offered me an interesting part in the movie."

"You mean the' Sammi Wray?" Sonny's eyes lit up like search beacons. "She's more than just beautiful. She's like the song *Poetry in Motion*. She doesn't just move; she sways like a wave out on the ocean, graceful as a ballerina, fluid as a summer breeze. If she's an angel, she's the highest angel from Heaven. She's high class, without a hint of snobbery. And smart!" Sonny raised his palms, "And her perfume scent is from a mythical garden. Eden? Shangri Las? El Dorado? A place only she can take me."

Spence, Penny, and Rick's jaws dropped. They looked at each other with raised eyebrows and tilted heads.

"Sonny!" Spence raised his hands. "I'm used to hearing you say 'awesome,' 'stoked,' 'bummer,' 'cowabunga,' or 'bodacious' every other word. Since when did you become Shakespeare?"

"Well, Sonny," Penny chuckled. "I found her impressive, and I surely can't remember a woman so captivating you."

"At last." Rick held up his glass of beer. "The great Sonny Dyer. California's Dan Juan and Casanova rolled into one." Rick chuckled. "The irrepressible Lothario," he raised his glass, "has met his match. To Sammi Wray." Rick tapped glasses with Spence and then Penny.

"I know you said you would discuss your acting proposal later." Spence kept his beer glass aloft. "But tell us a little bit so we can at least toast."

"The associate producer, Sonny's new flame Sammi, asked me to wait until we're at Dodger Stadium." Penny reached into her purse. "She gave me these." She held aloft two tickets.

Sonny took them from her. He sniffed them, hoping some of Sammi's aroma rubbed off on them. "Oh, my goodness! These are deluxe box seats!"

"He's right." Spence took the tickets from Sonny and perused them. "You can't buy these even if you had the money." He beamed at Penny. "Thank you." He kissed her. "Let's toast to the Dodgers, Koufax and Drysdale, and a 1963 World Series win."

Spence, Penny, Sonny, and Rick tapped glasses.

That night, Sonny paced back and forth. He squeezed his head. *'My black book. Yes. My black book.'* He rifled through his bureau drawer, finding it under a disordered pile of unpaid bills. *'Juanita, Kim, Sandi. Surely, one will come over.'* "Who the hell are you kidding, Sonny *Dyer?*" *'Sammi, Sammi, Sammi, Sammi.'* He closed his eyes. He smelled her perfumed body and tasted her silky skin.

Chapter 5

May 11, 1963

"Penny!" Spence beamed. "What magic did you work? I can't even sneak past the usher for a glance at the field from here, and here you got us tickets."

"The associate producer seems to want me." Penny smiled back at him. "I guess these tickets are her bribe."

"I don't know about that." Spence chuckled. "Since when does a producer need to bribe an unknown actress to take a movie part?"

"Well, seeing that I'm not an actress at all." Penny laughed. "Maybe that's why. Anyway, Spence, here's the scoop: it's only a dance scene. She wants me to dance with the star, Johnny Bright. Meanwhile, his girlfriend, Bernadette Hennesey, looks on and seethes with jealousy. Miss Wray said," Penny blushed and looked downward, "I was the only girl on the set pretty enough to make her jealous."

"Miss Wray has an exceptional eye. Tonight is Ladies' night." Spence kissed Penny's cheek. "And you're sure worth more than just a game ticket." He looked up at the cavernous five tiers of stands. "This place seats 56,000. Any seat next to you is the best seat in the house, even if it's up there." Spence pointed to the distant right field upper deck.

"Thank you, Spence." Penny blushed. "I love you."

Spence mumbled back, "I love you too." He looked away from her. "Hey, we got Sandy Koufax pitching tonight. When I say he's the best, I mean the best of the best."

"Now Spence," She rested her head on his shoulder. "How long have we been together? I know we seldom talk about sports." Penny chuckled. "But even a dumb blonde knows about Sandy Koufax." She looked at him with droopy eyes. "You don't think I'm a dumb blonde, do you?"

"What? You know I never thought of you that way. After all, you're better educated than me."

"Classroom." Penny smiled. "I need your degree from the school of hard knocks." She tapped the top of his head with her right knuckles.

"It's national anthem time." Spence and Penny stood.

"Play Ball!" The umpire bellowed.

"My goodness." Spence grinned. "We're close enough to hear the umpire!"

"Hey, It's Willie Mays! He's right in front of us." Penny smiled at Spence and pointed at the on-deck circle. "Sonny described Sammi Wray as poetry in motion. Can we use that line to describe how Willie Mays plays baseball?"

"Only if you can conjure Shakespeare, Dante, Keats, Whitman, and Dickinson. I gave you five great poets because Willie Mays is great at all five things one looks for in a ballplayer." Spence held up five fingers. "Hitting for average, hitting for power, speed, throwing arm, and fielding. If ever there existed a flawless player, it's Willie Mays."

Willie Mays stepped up to bat.

"Ouch!" Penny groaned. "Koufax just made him look like he's drinking coffee with a fork."

"That's the beauty of baseball," Spence chuckled, "It's a game of failure. If a batter only succeeds three out of the ten times he comes to bat, he's considered a star. If Sonny wiped out on seven of the ten waves he catches, he wouldn't even win a booby prize much less a professional title like the Malibu International."

"Yes, but if Koufax can strike out Willie Mays, he's the man. A little later, they will go again. Maybe Willie flips the script." Penny squeezed Spence's hand. "Now I understand why you love the game so much. It's both an individual and a team game. It pits the pitcher and batter in a one-on-one fight. But unlike boxing or wrestling, it involves an entire team."

"Each day you amaze me more, Penny." Spence raised her hand and kissed it. "I know it's wrong to assume you know little about baseball just because you're a woman. But you understand the game better than any guy I know."

"How soon you forget," Penny laughed and shook her head, "My father played for the Hollywood Stars of the Pacific Coast League. That's how he met my mom. While you were wrestling in Florida, I was the star of the Santa Monica High School softball team. I got an offer from UCLA, but, as you know, I am more interested in fashion design." Penny grinned. "Changing the subject, our friend, Sonny Dyer…you two make for a strange pairing. I mean, look at you," Penny leaned her forearms on Spence's shoulder and kissed his ear, "You're handsome, tall, and strong. You're even famous. But you're modest. I love you for that. But Sonny!" She threw her hands up. "He's full of himself, and he lets everyone know it."

"I understand him." Spence squeezed Penny's hand. "Yeah, he comes off as a bit arrogant."

"A bit?" Penny chuckled.

"Back in Florida, I wrestled with a guy named Johnny Durham. He was conceited and arrogant in the worst possible way. He was a bully and a bigot. He walked around like he was superior to everyone. Any positive feeling for his fellow man was limited to himself." Spence nodded. "Deep inside, you know Sonny has a good heart, and he doesn't have a bigoted bone in his body." Spence tapped his chest. "You know something, Penny? That other Johnny rubs me the wrong way too."

"You mean the movie star," Penny flicked her long blond hair, "Johnny Bright?"

"Yeah," Spence nodded, "Him. I hate to bad talk someone I have yet to speak with, nevertheless, I've seen how he treats everyone on the set. He acts like the extras are dead fish washed up on the beach. He listens to the director, Andrew Sparks, I guess he knows he must, but he treats the rest of his staff like dirt. There's something weird about him as well. Here he can pick and choose any of the hottest girls on the set…"

"Except one," Penny laughed.

"You're the best, Penny," Spence shook his head and chuckled, "and no one else is even a close second. "Yet if there is a close second, it's his costar, Bernadette Hennessy. She's the dream girl of many young men, but have you noticed? When Bright does a love scene with her, he seems detached."

"When our friend Sonny looks at Sammi," Penny laughed. "He's detached all right- detached from Planet Earth." Penny chuckled. "He sure fancies himself as quite the ladies' man. But I got a feeling our associate producer, Sammi Wray, is about to cut him down to size."

"I don't know if that's a good thing or a bad thing." Spence shrugged, "I mean, Sonny doesn't have a mean bone in his body, and he's devoid of prejudice. Yes. He's sure of himself. But he doesn't look down on anyone." Spence touched his temples. "Sometimes I think I'm the only one who sees that in him." He shook his head. "If I wasn't his best friend, God only knows how often he would have gotten his ass kicked."

"He's a lover, not a fighter." Penny beamed. "I hit the jackpot. I got myself a lover and a fighter." Spence and Penny kissed.

"Hey, there's a baseball game going on. How about I kiss you between the strikes and you kiss me between the…Um…on second thought, you mentioned Sammi Wray as *our* associate producer. Does that mean you're taking her offer?"

"Well, she says it will only take an afternoon. Why not?"

"If she'll give you tickets like this again, I say hell yes!"

"Okay, I'll do it." Penny pointed to the field. "Speaking of cutting people down to size, it didn't take long for Koufax to get the Giants out."

***

"Well, Spence, there's one out in the eighth. Are we allowed to say it?"

"That's a player's superstition." Spence chuckled. "Do you want me to say it, or do you want to say it?"

"I'll give you the honors." Penny pecked his cheek.

34

"Okay." Spence folded his hands behind his head. "Yes. Sandy Koufax is pitching a perfect game."

"The Giant's catcher, Ed Bailey, isn't giving in."

"I agree, Penny. He keeps fouling off Sandy's toughest pitches."

"Oh no." Penny grabbed Spence's arm and shook it. "He walked him. It's my fault. I shouldn't have said anything."

"Don't fret, Penny. He's still working on a no-hitter."

"Hey! Hush." Penny put her finger over Spence's lips. "Do you want to jinx him?"

"Look at that! First pitch, groundball to the shortstop. That's one." Spence held up his pointer finger. "That's two." He held up two fingers. "Double play! That didn't take Koufax long. He's faced the minimum number of batters, and the no-hitter is intact."

"We're winning eight to nothing. I hope the Dodgers make three quick outs. I can't wait to see Koufax finish the no-hitter."

***

"We're one batter away." Spence nervously shook his fists. "Uh oh. It's going to be a tough one. Willie McCovey is coming to bat. He leads the league in home runs."

"I can see why." Penny looked at the batter's box. "He's almost as big as our Frank Howard."

"And he hits 'em just as far."

"He walked him." Penny smiled. "I guess that's a good thing, seeing how McCovey is such a dangerous hitter."

"I hate to disagree with you, Penny. We want Koufax to get a no-hitter. The man coming to the plate," Spence pointed to the field, "Harvey Kuenn. He doesn't hit home runs like Willie McCovey, but he's a tougher out. Harvey Kuenn recently won the American League batting title by hitting over .350. And he seldom strikes out."

"Look at that!" Penny pointed to the field. "It's a grounder to the second baseman." Penny beamed. Dodger Stadium erupted. "He's out! Koufax did it! No-hitter! We got to witness history!"

The Dodgers swarmed to the pitcher's mound to congratulate Sandy Koufax. Spence and Penny hugged and kissed.

Chapter 6

The shrill ring of his telephone awoke Sonny Dyer. "Dammit." He mumbled. "Five am. Who the hell?" He glanced at the girl who shared his bed for the night. *'You're slipping Sonny; you're slipping. At least the phone didn't wake her up.'* He held the receiver to his right ear. "Yeah. Who's calling me at five bloody am in the morning?"

"It's Myrna Myers. I'm one of Sammi Wray's assistants. There's good surf at Malibu. Be there no later than eight am. We're doing the shoot."

He crept into his bathroom. Imagining Sammie Wray disrobing invigorated him. After a hasty shower, it pointed to him shaving. "Ouch," He nicked himself.

He dressed and tiptoed out of his apartment, not awakening his partner from the night before.

***

Several beefy guards were the first layer surrounding the beach scene. Two boom microphones were the next layer. Finally, two cameras on a dolly track and a main camera on a technician's shoulder made for the outside layer. A good-looking, tanned male intern instructed Sonny to join a group of young men and women sitting on the beach. Sonny paid them scant attention. He scanned every inch of the set. He gasped. His heart skipped a beat. Stylish Birkenstock sandals enhanced the flow of her thin ankles to shapely calves to narrow knees. Her cotton, light pastel-patterned, flared skirt ended inches above her knees. A subdued burgundy belt circled her narrow waist. Her crisp white silk blouse was opened just enough to reveal the natural perfection of her bust. Bright red lips seemed to frame white teeth set straight as ivory keys on a concert piano. A silk scarf matching her skirt secured the top of her black hair. A gentle breeze caused the scarf and the ends of her tress to flutter. Oversized, black sunglasses sat on her thin nose. Sonny licked his lips and stared at her, hoping Sammi would notice him.

"Sit here." The director's assistant pushed down on his shoulder.

Sonny looked around. Bernadette Hennessey sat separately from the group. She played a teenager in the movie, yet he could see she was much older and more mature. *'My teenage crush. I'm finally seeing her in person. Why does it not matter?'*

Johnny Bright, carrying a guitar, walked onto the set and keeled in front of the group. He strummed three chords and lip-synched a love ballad for Bernadette.

'Bernadette is flashing just the right smile,' Sonny thought. 'But something is wrong with his smile. It seems too forced.'

"Hey! Great song, Johnny!" A tall, slender young man stood. "But let's surf!"

"Cut!" The director shouted. "Let's take scene two."

The young assistant clasped Sonny's arm. "Grab a surfboard, you're on."

Surfboards under arms, Sonny and Johnny walked toward the ocean.

"So, you're my surfing body double." Johnny licked his lips. "I like to get to know who's playing me." He gazed into Sonny's eyes.

'Body double?' Spence snapped his head away from Johnny, 'What's he talking about? He's nothing like me:

taller, thinner, and blond. Rather than a surfer, he looks more like someone from a Nazi propaganda poster.'

"What do you say we share a beer in my trailer after we finish shooting?

"Yeah, Sure thing, Buddy."

"Buddy?" Johnny put his left hand on his hip. "That's a new one. Yeah sure, we can be buddies." He cracked a smile. "I'll have a cold beer waiting for you in my trailer after the shoot."

* * *

Sonny paddled furiously and stood on his surfboard while sliding down the face of an overhead-sized wave. *'A bit larger than a wave for hotdogging, but if anyone can pull this off, it's you, Sonny.'* Sonny walked to the nose of his board and curled his toes over the edge. *'Hope you're watching, Sammi.'* He shuffled back to the board's center, performed a radical pivot and re-entry, and then did a handstand. He rode to the wave's shoulder, took the white water to shore, and ran onto the beach. He spotted the director nodding and smiling.

The intern greeted him. "Great job, Mr. Dyer." He put a towel over Sonny's shoulder. "You did exactly what Mr. Sparks wanted."

"What's your name, kid?"

"Cory."

'Good looking kid. A little young, but he might make a good wingman in picking up chicks.' Sonny glanced over Cory's shoulder. 'Oh my God! It's her! She's smiling at me.' "Excuse me, kid." He sprinted over to Sammi. "Well, what did you think?"

Sammi smiled. "I think you're quite a surfer." She took off her sunglasses. "I recommended you to Mr. Feldman. You looked good, and you made me look good."

Sonny looked into her brown eyes. His nerves tingled with the fluttering of her eyelashes. "Well, you'll look even better on my arm tonight." Sonny inhaled deeply. "What do you say to dinner tonight?"

"Dinner? Where?" Sammi laughed and put her sunglasses back on. "Chico's Taco Stand? What's on the wine list? Lucky Lager?"

Sonny blanched.

"Look, you did a great job today." Sammi reached out and placed her hand on Sonny's shoulder."

Sonny looked at her hand and panted.

"You're a good-looking kid and an outstanding surfer." She put her sunglasses back on. "I can't see any of my extras turning you down. As for Bernadette and me, I think it's best you stay in your lane and stick to your age."

Sonny's voice took a higher pitch and softer volume, "But I've dated older women." He opened his palms and leaned forward.

"I'm sure you have." Sammi laughed. "I again thank you for an outstanding surfing performance. I'm sure Mr. Sparks and Mr. Feldman appreciate getting it in one take. You're done for the day. We'll call you when or if we need you. Now, if you will excuse me, I have much to do." She smiled at him. "Good luck, Mr. Dyer." She walked over to Myrna Myers, took a clipboard from her, and perused it.

Sonny felt his spirits sink like the Titanic.

Chapter 7

Sonny lurched through his flat's front door. *'At least what's her name didn't stick around.'* He saw a perfumed note with a lipstick mark on his night table. Spence crumpled it and threw it into his wastebasket. He sat on his bed, put his chin in his palm, and closed his eyes. He imagined Sammi. Her hair and scarf fluttered in the breeze. *'It's way too early, but you caused this, Sammi.'* Sonny rifled through his night table drawer and found it. He grabbed a flask and downed its contents. "Hah," he shook his head and groaned as the bourbon burned his throat. Sitting back down, he tilted back his head. A vision of Sammi's breasts cloaked in gossamer white silk, her crimson lips, ivory teeth…The shrill ring of his phone. "Let it be her." He steepled his hands. "Please be her." Hastily, he placed the receiver to his ear. "Hello!"

"Sonny Dyer?" A male voice.

"Yes." Sonny dropped his chin to his chest.

"It's Robert Shipman from Hang Ten Swimwear. We got the news that a Hollywood movie is featuring you surfing."

"Yes." Sonny sat up. "Beach Party USA. We finished the shoot this morning."

"Excellent. Look, winning the Malibu International has already made you more marketable. Appearing in a Hollywood motion picture with Johnny Bright and Bernadette Henesey will lift your brand name even more. Let's secure a deal. Can you meet me in my downtown office at four o'clock?

Sonny stood up and smiled. "Sure." He pictured himself showing Sammi the new contract. "I'll be there."

***

Robert Shipman's secretary showed Sonny into his office. Sonny looked back at her, winked, and pantomimed a kiss as he entered. She blushed and lowered her head before closing the door.

"Hey, good to see you, Mr. Dyer." The middle-aged Robert Shipman had slicked back his thin, gray-tipped hair; he wore a white collared shirt and black necktie. He stood, walked around his desk, and shook Sonny's hand. "Have a seat." He motioned to a chair positioned in front of his desk. Robert returned to his seat behind his desk. "It's right there in front of you. Have a look."

Sonny picked up the contract and read it. "The deal is exactly as written." Robert smiled. "We are doubling the money and length of your sponsorship. However, it is conditional on your name being in the Beach Party USA credits."

"I have no problem with that." Sonny took a pen from Mr. Shipman's desk.

"Sign on the dotted line." Shipman pointed to the contact.

Sonny signed.

***

Sonny ran into Studio 7. He clutched a copy of his new Hang Ten Swimwear sponsorship contract as a gold certificate. It took three minutes for him to spot Sammi. She stood with Myna Myers and another assistant. "Sammi! Sammi!" He ran up to her.

"What are you doing here?"

"I came to show you this." He put his Hang Ten sponsorship contract in front of Sammi.

"You're not supposed to be here." She moved his wrist away with her fingertips. "Once your role is complete, you're no longer authorized to be on set."

Sonny gasped. "What do you mean?"

"Things are chaotic enough around here without you getting in the way. Time is money. We can only make room for working cast and crew."

"Okay. I understand. Look," he again held up the contract. "I was a star surfer before you hired me. Now you've made me even more of a star. Let me take you to dinner. Any restaurant of your choice. Cost is no object."

Sammie sighed and lowered her shoulders. "I'm flattered. I said before, you're a handsome and talented young man. You'll get your break, and you'll find the right girl."

"But this is my break, and you are the right girl." Sonny flashed her his best smile.

Sammi pursed her lips in a straight line. "I would hardly call a woman my age a girl."

"But that's what I find so attractive in you." He raised his palms. "The others are more like playmates. Each time I'm with one of them, I still feel empty. You're mature, strong, and smart—a real woman. You're what's missing from my life."

"Thank you. I'm flattered. But what makes you think I'm missing something, and I need a surfer boy to fill it?"

Sonny's jaw dropped. He turned pale.

"Look, Mr. Dyer, I've dealt with every one of your kind. Whether it's a cute surfer, ball player, actor, or musician, you're used to getting what you want. When you don't get it, you think you're entitled to it. Look, I like you. You're a decent enough kid, but I must produce a movie. Now, if you would excuse me, I need to get back to work, and you," she pointed at him, "must leave the set. You are no longer authorized to be here."

"But you made me a star." Sonny felt his voice fade. He felt detached from his body. "You're putting my name in lights." He spread his palms. "What more can you ask for?"

"I don't think you understand," Sammi looked at her clipboard. "Didn't your agent tell you? We hired you as Johnny Bright's stunt double. You also signed a non-disclosure agreement."

"A non-disclosure agreement?" Johnny shrugged. "What are you talking about?"

"We superimposed Johnny's image over yours for the surfing scenes. You agreed in writing not to reveal that it was you. Therefore, we can't include your name in the credits lest someone puts one and one together."

"What about my speaking role?"

"'Surf's up' is not exactly a Shakespearean soliloquy. Mr. Sparks decided to use Nick Anderson. He's appeared in other beach party movies as part of Johnny and Bernadette's clique."

"But my sponsorship agreement depends on…"

Sammi put up her hand like a policeman's halt. "Go back and talk with your agent. I don't have time to argue. Keeping in our good graces will improve your chances of us giving you a break later. Please leave by yourself, or I'll have security escort you from the premises." Sammi turned and walked away.

Sonny froze like a statue. Unable to think, the set noise bounced about his skull. He breathed in short gasps. With blurry vision, he took one long, last look at Sammi. *'She's not looking back. Don't make it worse. Better get out of here.'* He trudged off the set.

Chapter 8

The Contours, a six-man rhythm and blues singing group, wore matching orange swim trunks and matching orange tropical shirts with green palm trees. The six black men stood in the sand of the makeshift Studio 7 beach. A film of the Pacific Ocean played in the background. Fourteen young white females sat in front of them. Sitting separately were fourteen young white males. Johnny Bright and Bernadette Hennesey sat three meters away from the males. Director Sparks shouted, "Lights, sound, action."

The Contours' lead singer, Joseph Billingslea, moved his lips to a recording of his speaking voice. "Nineteen-sixty-four and we gonna dance some more. You gotta keep up with the time, if you wanna be mine. So, if you can do it, let me know it."

The record advanced to the backing singers lip synching, "Do it, do it, do it." A brief instrumental break. "Do it, do it, do it."

The lead singer lip-synched, "I went to a dance, just the other night."

The five backing singers turned right and left while moving their arms and snapping their fingers in harmony, lip-synching, "Other night, other night, other night."

The lead singer, "The dance they were doin' there, it was out of sight."

The backing singers, "Out-a-sight, out-a-sight, out-a-sight."

The lead singer, "I knew right away, yeah, that there was nothing to it."

The backing singers, "Nothin' to it, nothin' to it, nothin' to it."

The lead singer, "I could tell right away, oh boy, even I could do it."

The backing singers, "I could do it; I could do it; I could do it."

The lead singer, "First step: you move to your left."

The females and males got up and danced solo to the steps that the Contours' lead singer sang.

The lead singer, "Second step: you gotta go for yourself. Third step: You're doin' alright."

The backing singers, "Oh, oh, oh, oh, oh, oh, oh, oh!"

The lead singer, "Grab yourself a partner, then you start it movin' too."

Each male took a female by the hand and danced with her.

The lead singer, "To and fro, to and fro."

Johnny stood. Bernadette grabbed Johnny's arm. He yanked it away and strutted toward the group.

The lead singer, "The next thing you know, hey, you want to do it some more."

Johnny took Penny's hand and pulled her from her male dance partner. Penny wore a yellow Bikini with white dots bordering the top and bottom edges. Johnny wore red swim trunks with a white line on the sides. He took Penny's hand and twirled her around. After facing her, he held both of her hands. They twisted their hips while lowering into a full squat and twisted as they rose. Johnny pulled her in. He braced one arm around her torso and tilted her back. Her blonde tress cascaded back like water poured from a vessel.

The camera panned to Bernadette. She frowned, bit her lip, and furrowed her eyebrows.

Johnny spun Penny again. They stood beside each other, held hands, and raised them together before pulling apart and fast dancing to the rest of the song. They shuffled their feet and moved their arms in a swimming motion. Penny shook her head, splaying her hair.

At the end of the recording, the Contours bowed to the cheering audience. Johnny and Penny looked at each other and applauded. The camera then focused on Bernedette glaring with arms folded and frowning with her lower lip over her upper lip.

"Cut!" The director shouted.

"Great job, Penny." Johnny nodded. "Cory," Johnny shouted to the young male intern. "Bring me a towel." The intern ran over and draped a towel over Johnny's shoulder. "Thank you." Johnny put his arm around Cory's waist and squeezed before walking to talk with the director.

Arthur Feldman stood outside his office. He beckoned to Myrna Myers, "Miss Myers, get Penny Williams." He pointed at her, "Have her see me in my office."

Penny stood alone. She scanned the studio, hoping to find Spence. Bernadette walked over and faced Penny. *'She's shorter than I expected, a little older too, but what expressive eyes and charisma.'* Penny's nerves jittered.

"Don't worry." Bernadette smiled disarmingly. "I don't bite."

"Thanks." Penny breathed a sigh of relief. "It's just that, well, you're a…"

"A star?" Bernadette continued to smile. "A celebrity?"

"Well, yes." Penny blushed and lowered her head.

"I just wanted to thank you for making my job easier."

Penny skewed her head and shrugged.

"I was tasked to seethe in jealousy when my boyfriend abandoned me to dance with you." Bernadette placed her hand on Penny's shoulder. "You made it easy. Look at you. You're gorgeous. You make me jealous for real." She chuckled.

Penny blushed.

"My idea was for you to be a vixen who steals Johnny rather than a friendly all-American gal that he happens to choose." Bernadette laughed. "But do I have a say? I may be a star, but I'm far from the center of the Hollywood galaxy."

"Is Johnny your boyfriend for real?"

"No." Bernadette guffawed. "That's what the publicists want everyone to believe. More for his sake than mine." She sniggered. "Keep this secret." Bernadette put her finger over her lips. "I'm married. My husband is a heart surgeon. And by the looks of things, you're gonna break a few and give him some business." She laughed and squeezed Penny's hand.

"I'm no heartbreaker." Penny blushed and lowered her head.

"Maybe not in real life. You may from the silver screen. This is my last beach party movie. I hate to say it, but I'm getting too old to play a teenager. Besides, I'll get typecast if

I make any more of these flicks. It's an easy role. I think you can take my place."

"But I'm no actress."

"You don't have to act. Just be yourself. Your looks and charisma will do the rest. After all, these beach party movies are far from Citizen Kane or Gone With the Wind." Bernadette held both of her hands. "Take the opportunity now. Times are changing. I don't know if this genre will float with the public much longer."

"Excuse me." Myrna Myers arrived. "But, Miss Williams, the producer wants to see you in his office."

"You better go." Bernadette winked. "He is the big boss."

Myna moved her head toward Arthur Feldman's office. "Follow me."

***

The crew members moved props on and off the set. They set up six mock-ups of chopper motorcycles on the edge of the sand. Spence, Rick, and four other actors stood by. They were dressed in leather boots, denim jeans, and leather vests.

***

Johnny Bright was in his private dressing room. "Cory. Get me my turquoise trunks." The intern hustled through clothes hanging from a rack.

"Will these do?" Cory held up a pair of turquoise swim trunks with a small white embroidery of a surfer on the right leg.

"Yes." Johnny took the trunks from the intern. "Perfect for the fight scene." Johnny held eye contact with Cory while stripping out of his red trunks and donning the turquoise trunks.

***

"You look nervous, Rick."

"Come on, Spence, you fake fight under lights for a living. This is a first for me."

"When I wrestle, I work with dudes as big as dinosaurs, and many of them know how to fight for real." Spence opened his hands. "These guys are just a bunch of skinny actors."

"It's not that." Rick had mounted the prop chopper motorcycle. "I want to do a good job and not mess up the scene."

"You'll do fine."

"Are you guys ready?" A crew member asked. Two crew members each grabbed a Scorpion member's bike. The sound system played heavy electric guitar music.

The actor playing Zach Zurlien yelled, "Let's get 'em gang!"

The crew gave their prop motorcycles a running push.

"Hey, boys," Johnny Bright pointed to the ocean. "The waves are rocking and rolling!"

The sound system played engine rumble noise. The Scorpion gang rolled between Johnny Bright and the ocean.

Zach Zurlein disembarked his motorcycle. "The only thing that's gonna rock is us, and all that's gonna roll is your head." He threw a punch at Johnny. He blocked it and countered with a punch to Zach's gut. He groaned and keeled over. Spence ran over. Johnny slugged him in the mouth.

Shock waves accompanied Spence's teeth rattling. He tasted salty, acrid blood.

Next, Johnny slugged Spence in the midsection. It failed to affect him, although Spence knew he intended to hurt him. Spence followed the script and bent over while holding his gut for Johnny to strike his jaw with an uppercut. Spence saw sparks as he followed the script and fell on his back. He watched Johnny fight other Scorpion gang members with pulled punches.

***

"Good afternoon, Miss Williams." Arthur Feldman closed and locked the door behind him and pointed at a couch. He sat behind his desk and placed his palms on the desktop. "You can call me Arthur if I may call you Penny." The producer smiled asymmetrically and narrowed his eyes. "I'm not the only one that you've impressed." He slid his hands forward, palms down. "Mr. Sparks, Miss Wray, and others see what I see." He rapidly blinked. "A beautiful and talented young woman. You're a natural, and your camera charisma will take you a long way."

Penny sat at the edge of the couch. She gripped her knees and stiffened her shoulders. Wearing only a yellow bikini and no towel, she felt a chill.

"You're better than most, much better even." He grinned and lowered his head to focus on her breasts. "But you're not the only one. You do know that I can make or break you. You have no experience, but I can hire Hollywood's best acting coaches to get you up to speed. This is the final beach party movie of Bernadette Hennesey's contract. She has elected not to renew. These movies are cheap and fast to make. I want to make at least one more before the culture inevitably shifts and they become passe."

Penny fidgeted with her fingers. *'He's looking right through me.'* She looked away.

"You're greener to this business than anyone I've ever offered a starring role." He narrowed his eyes, only opening them halfway. He held an asymmetrical smirk, his right lip slightly curled. He looked her up and down.

Penny put one hand over her crotch and the other over her chest.

"You need to understand that this business has certain protocols. Follow them and I'll make you a star. Fail to honor our little tradition and you remain an obscurity." The producer stood and walked over to the couch.

*****

"Cut." The director yelled. "I like it, but I want another take. Carter, you're a professional wrestler. I want you to coach the other Scorpions on how to sell getting hit."

'The son-of-a-bitch can't even see that I'm bleeding for real.' "Cory," Spence yelled to the intern.

The intern looked toward Spence.

"Cory, please bring me a towel."

"Are you alright, Mr. Carter?" He handed Spence a towel.

"I'll be fine." Spence held the towel over his bleeding mouth. He noticed that Johnny Bright had joined them. "What the hell, man?" Spence showed him the bloody towel. "This was only a movie scene. Don't tell me that it was accidental. In wrestling, we call an accident of this sort a potato. The other wrestler must apologize, or it becomes a shoot. By shoot, I don't mean a camera shoot. You don't want me in a shoot."

"Cool it, man." Johnny grinned. "I thought a big boy like you might like it rough." He licked his lips and winked at Spence.

"No. I prefer to work like a professional." He prodded. "You may have leaps and bounds more experience in movies, nevertheless, I know hell-of-a-lot more about professionalism than you."

"Hey," he stepped forward and laid his right hand on Spence's shoulder. "I was only trying to help you."

Spence knocked his hand away. "What the hell are you talking about?"

"I could tell that Penny likes it rough, but you don't know how to give it to her." Johnny folded his arms and smirked. "I just gave you a much-needed lesson. Why don't you come to my trailer and thank me over a beer."

"You son-of-a-bitch." Spence slugged Johnny's jaw.

"You hit me!" He staggered back and massaged his jaw. "You hit me."

"You stupid bastard." Andrew Sparks ran over to Johnny and looked him over before confronting Spence. "If you hurt him, so much as put a bruise on him, or caused swelling, or anything else preventing him from working, you're going to reimburse me for every penny of every second of delay."

"With what?" Spence prodded back.

"So that's how you want it?" The director hunched his shoulders. "Security. Give this man a lesson in respect."

Spence turned around. His first sight was Rick Drasich decking a security guard. Spence moved next to Rick. Both went into fists raised, fighting stances. The security guards ignored their fallen comrade and surrounded them.

"Cory! Cory!" Johnny Bright sat up. "Help me."

The intern moved next to Johnny.

"Rub my jaw." As Cory rubbed his jaw, Johnny put his arm around him and nibbled on his fingers. "I'm all right." Johnny pointed at the security guards. "Just get them out of here."

The Security guards escorted Rick and Spence toward the exit.

Andrew Sparks yelled, "You two will never, ever again, work in movies, not even as a janitor."

***

"Come on, baby," the producer climbed on top of Penny, grabbed her wrists, pinned her shoulders to the couch, and started kissing her. "You know you want to be a star. You know what you must do to be one."

The odor of his tobacco-laced breath gave Penny a burst of energy and an adrenaline rush. She knocked Felman's right arm away and spat on him.

"You bitch!" He wiped away her spit before again grabbing her wrists. He overpowered her, pinning her arms back against the couch.

"No! No!" She shook her head.

Feldman tore off her pearl necklace, lacerating the back of her neck, and tossed the necklace aside. Pearls bounced about the floor like dried peas in a boiling pot.

"No!" Tears streamed from her eyes

He again pinned her wrists and planted kisses on her cheeks.

"No! No! No!"

The producer sneered at her objections and angrily bit her neck like a vampire, drawing blood.

Penny screamed and bit the side of his face.

He let go of her left wrist to touch his cheek. Glowering at her, he slapped her face.

Tendrils of pain shot through Penny.

He released one hand from her wrists, tore off her bikini top, and threw it against the wall. He leered at her naked breasts. "Lovely. Lovely. Lovely." He pinched her nipples with wrench-like force, "Titty, titty, twisty, twisty," he spoke in a creepy, infantile voice as he twisted her nipples like turning thumbscrews. "Te he he," he giggled.

The torture drove Penny to near blackout. She saw multiple images of her screaming, convoluted face revolving like on a Ferris wheel.

"Ha! Ha! Ha!" The producer's laugh sounded like it came from the gates of Hell. He released her left wrist, reached under her bikini bottom, and digitally violated her. He pinched his forefinger and thumb together while inside of her.

The agony caused her body to shake in involuntary spasms.

"We're only beginning, deary. You had your chance to play by the rules. Now I've changed the game." He opened his mouth and lowered his head toward her breasts.

With a burst of awareness and adrenaline, Penny elbowed his temple.

"Uhh." He groaned and clutched his head.

Penny shot her right leg upward, striking his privates with her shin.

The producer groaned and rolled off her. "Ugh," he scrunched into a fetal position.

Penny got up and ran to the door. Locked. She twisted the knob and pulled to no avail. She fell to her knees and vainly tried to twist the knob. Feldman climbed to his feet and lunged at her. Trousers around his ankles, he tripped. Penny spotted a small latch and flicked it. The door opened. She ran out screaming. The producer, trousers still around his ankles, chased her onto the set.

"Spence!"

"What the…" Spence ran to her. They hugged. He kept his arms around her so no one could see her breasts. "Cory!" He yelled at the intern. "Get her a towel."

The intern grabbed a towel, hustled over, and handed it to him. Spence wrapped it around Penny. He spotted Feldman, trousers around his ankles. Anger surged through Spence's veins…*A flash of himself covered in hair, muscles taut like steel cables but wired unlike any human. He brandished a calcified animal femur bone as a weapon…* He roared like a beast, lifted the producer overhead, and slammed him with extreme prejudice to the concrete floor. He cocked his leg to kick him.

"Spence." Penny ran over and hugged him. He put his arm around her and looked at the fallen producer.

"Ugh, ugh, ugh," the producer gasped for air. Blood dripped from his mouth and nose. His body went stiff. His eyes no longer moved. He wheezed with each gasp for breath.

"Oh my God! What the hell is going on here?" Andrew Sparks ran to the scene. "You again!" He prodded at Spence. The director gazed at the fallen producer. "What the hell! Get medical! Fast! Call an ambulance!" Sparks turned to Spence and prodded. "Don't move. The police are on their way. You can watch my movie while locked up in San Quentin." Myrna Myers, mouth agape and lips circled, joined the scene. "Miss Myers." He pointed at her. "Call the police. Get them here right away."

"Yes, Myrna." Spence looked at her. "Call the police." He squeezed Penny. "I'm going to press charges against your producer for rape." He turned to the director. "That's right, Sparks." Spence prodded. "You and Feldman are powerful men. But you're not Al Capone, and Sixties LA is not Twenties Chicago. You don't own every newspaper, D.A., and judge in town." Spence kept Penny covered while he looked at the cast and crew who joined the scene. "Not every witness here will perjure themselves. Not for what you're paying them. Feldman already has a reputation. This time he went too far. Your reputation is sunk just by association. Everyone will know what Feldman did. This movie is finished. Forever!"

Penny embraced Spence and bawled.

"Gawwwd Dammit, you! This isn't over."

"You're right, when we're all in San Quentin, I'll finish the job on you," Spence wielded his fist, "and make sure the other inmates do to Feldman what he tried on Penny."

“Okay. So, none of us presses charges.” Sparks prodded. “But get the hell out! Get out! And stay out! None of you will ever work in show business again. After we’re done with you,” He prodded, “you won’t even get hired shoveling elephant shit at a circus.”

Spence held Penny tighter. Blood dripped from her right nipple and a blood droplet was on her inner thigh. He kept the towel around her breasts while using its edge to wipe the tears from her eyes. He walked her out. Rick walked with them, eyeballing anyone thinking of stopping them.

Chapter 9

Sonny drove his yellow Deuce Coupe southbound on the Pacific Coast Highway to Huntington Beach and the Mysticurl Open surfing contest. 'I'm only up against locals. Normally, I wouldn't bother with it.' He scratched his head. 'But once Shipman at Hang Ten finds out I lost my speaking role, had Johnny Bright's image superimposed over mine, and had my name expunged from the credits… I'd best bring as many titles as possible.' He saw a couple hitchhiking. 'A brunette. Hair just below the shoulders,' He slowed down and took a long look. 'Not even close.' He sped up. 'Sammi, Sammi,' The intensity of his imagination recalled a hyacinth aroma; he rubbed his hand over his cheek and felt her smooth skin… "Dammit!" Sonny punched the steering wheel while passing his exit.

***

Sonny zipped into a parking space, toted his surfboard under his arm, and jogged onto the beach. Temporary loudspeakers broadcast a local radio station, *'Small time show; small time atmosphere'*. Sonny ignored the music and the disc jockey as he walked over to the entrants' table and signed in. Temporary wooden stands were at the back of the beach. Some spectators sat on the beach while most watched from Huntington Beach Pier. The judge's box was an elevated stand behind the entrant's table. *'Uh oh, Fritz Fisher. I stole his fiancée, Becky Blythe. I didn't have to do much. She came on to me. I did him a favor. I don't know why he didn't see it that way. Jeff Dill. He used to be my friend until I took what he thought was his wave at the Malibu International.'*

Sonny got lost in thought. 'What a drag. Breaking a friendship over that? Oh, and that's his sister, Lori. She blames me for her brother's loss. I asked her out three times. She snubbed me each time. He made eye contact with her. Lori looked away. 'Earth to Lori. I'm a better surfer than your loser brother. Mmm… you're not Sammi, but you still do look good. My offer for a date still stands.' Sonny looked at the man seated next to her. 'Oh, if it's not James Rodgers. I can't help it if your sponsorship offer sucked. Now I'm going to show you how much I'm worth.'

Sonny stood beside his surfboard and studied the waves. *'Too small. But I got a whole set of tricks for slop surf.'* He eyed a brunette sunning herself away from the contest area. *'Oh my God! Is it her?'* The loudspeaker played *'Our Day Will Come'* by Ruby and the Romantics. Sonny held his surfboard upright and closed his eyes. *He walked hand in hand with Sammi on the shoreline. They turned and faced each other. Warm seawater flowed over their ankles. He looked deeply into her lucid brown eyes.*

"Our first heat is Cameron Calhoun, Bob Garner, Sonny Dyer, and Pete Sharky." Cameron, Bob, and Pete ran into the ocean and paddled to the surf line.

Slow-breaking, overhead surf broke behind them, tinted orange by the setting sun. They embraced and kissed. Her delightful tongue sent delirious surges throughout his… Sonny opened his eyes and realized that the woman was not her.

"You better paddle out, Dyer." A contest official walked up to him. Sonny sprinted to the surf and joined the competitors.

***

"This is it. Last heat." The master of ceremonies announced over the loudspeaker. "Group One. Grab your boards! Surf's up!"

Sonny paddled out to just beyond the surf line. He scanned the horizon and saw a set of three sea swells rolling toward him. *'The second one is it. I got this contest in the bag. Time to put an exclamation point on it.'*

Sonny caught the set's second wave. He rode into the trough, gritted his teeth, and performed a radical 360-degree re-entry. He saw the audience applaud. He then hung ten for good measure. *'Time to seal the deal.'* He did a handstand.

The shrill of a ship's horn. "That's it." The MC announced. "The contest is over. All surfers come ashore. The judges will compile their scores and determine the winner."

***

Sonny sat cross-legged on the beach. Several people in the audience tapped his shoulder and congratulated him.

"Our third-place winner…Let's hear it for…Cameron Calhoun."

The audience clapped as a woman wearing a sundress and wide-brimmed sunhat handed Cameron a trophy.

"Our first runner-up. He comes all the way from Australia…Oscar Marlon!"

Sonny stood up and brushed off sand. He did his best to straighten his hair without a comb.

"Our winner didn't have to fly from Australia. He's a true Californian. Ladies and gentlemen. Our winner…"

Sonny scanned the beach for the prettiest girl. 'I sure wish Sammi could see me accept the trophy.'

"...Scott Young!" The audience cheered as a lean young man with curly brown hair stepped onto the podium and claimed his first-place trophy.

Sonny let his surfboard fall onto the sand. He stood still, jaw agape, and stared at Scott accepting his trophy. Sonny looked at the judges. *'He smirked at me. I swear, Fisher smirked at me. The jerk must not be over Becky. They plotted against me. It's a conspiracy.'*

Scott had walked off stage and came to Sonny.

"Where's Spence?" Scott confronted Sonny. "He may bail you out of fights, but he can't help you win a surfing contest." He pushed his trophy inches from Sonny's face. "Loser!" Scott and his girlfriend guffawed. "Ha! Ha! Ha!"

Sonny stood still. He slumped. His tenor plunged to Mariana Trench depth.

Chapter 10

"Show Mr. Carter in."

The secretary, a frail middle-aged woman, adjusted her horn-rimmed glasses while looking at the intercom. "Yes, Mr. Beck." She turned to Spence. "He's ready for you."

Simon Beck looked blankly over Spence's forehead. He said nothing and didn't gesture for Spence to sit.

After thirty tense seconds, Spence broke the silence, "You know why I'm here. My movie role is finished." He opened his hands. "I'm ready to renew our deal."

"Our Deal?" Beck placed his steepled hands on the desk. "I was not aware that we had a deal."

"You know." Spence took three deep breaths. "Extend the deal that we had." He slumped his shoulders. "You approved of me leaving my prior contract early to make a movie."

"The deal we had, as you so eloquently put it…" He raised his steepled hands and shook them at Spence, "…is, as you said, prior, meaning past tense." Beck folded his hands and placed them on his desk. "First, let's discuss your movie role. You punched the star. You topped that Flying Dutchman Overture off by body-slamming the producer and putting him in intensive care." Beck tilted his head. "Why you aren't in jail facing a lengthy prison term, I do not know."

"Sir, he violated my girlfriend with injury." Spence prodded. "Feldman's the one who should be in prison. The entire studio saw Penny run from his office topless. Feldman chased her with his pants around his ankles and then slipped them off."

"That shows how little you know. Perhaps you've never heard of the casting couch?"

"Penny didn't even want to be in the movie. She was fleeing. I wish you knew the extent of her trauma. She isn't even talking. I was defending her."

"Defending her virtue," Beck smirked. "I see. You think your girlfriend is above certain compromises to be a star. When you found out she was no different from the others, you figured slamming the producer would change it?"

"Dammit Beck." Spence stepped forward. "I know Penny." He prodded. "You don't. I was defending her from a rapist."

"A rapist? A rich and powerful producer who can get any starlet he wants." Beck gritted his teeth and shook his head. "Arguing with you is pointless." Beck stood. "Here's your dose of reality. Universal Entertainment owns United International Pictures. They also own 49.9 percent of the Western Wrestling Alliance. We have the final word, but they hold tremendous sway over our operation. Sparks and Feldman have mega power in the entertainment industry." Beck folded his arms. "I hope you figured out by now that professional wrestling is entertainment. Universal Entertainment has asked that I bar you from the territory."

Spence blanched. "You don't have to do it, do you?"

"No." Beck folded his hands behind his head. "But give me one reason why I should defy the people who butter my bread?"

"I make you money."

"Do you know who makes people money and makes it for powerful people?"

Spence shrugged.

"Johnny Bright."

"But he's…"

"Get in the real world. The entertainment industry only cares about the bottom line. In the movies, time is money. UIP has gobs of money invested in Johnny Bright. You and your bigoted temper put their investment at risk." Simon Beck put his palms on the table. "I've paid you more than you were ever worth." Beck slid his palms down and smirked. "Okay, I have a way of keeping you in my territory and keeping Feldman's people happy. I can re-sign you as a jobber. That, of course, will entail jobber pay." Beck grinned. "You'll have to move to a smaller apartment in a less desirable location, but at least, thanks to me, you will eat."

"You bastard!" Spence lurched forward.

"Don't even think about it." Beck prodded. "Security is right outside my office. My secretary has the police on speed dial. You won't get off as easy as you did with UIP." Beck steepled his fingers and sat up straight. "I take it that's a 'no'? We're done here. Please close the door behind you as you leave." Simon Beck waved toward the door. "Security will escort you from the premises."

Chapter 11

Dusk had retreated into its netherworld. The moon hid between the Earth and the Sun, forcing Spence to walk along the Santa Monica beach shoreline in darkness. He spotted a shadowy figure about a hundred meters ahead of him. *'He's staggering about like a drunk.'* Spence stopped walking to look closer. *'Why do I think I know that guy?'* Spence walked toward him. *'His height and build look familiar.'* He walked four steps closer. "Sonny?"

The figure drank from a flask. "Spence? How did you find me here?"

"I wasn't looking for you." Spence walked up to him. "Maybe it's karma, fate, or whatever, well, I found you." Spence craned his head forward. "You look terrible."

"Thanks, buddy." Sonny sipped from the flask, "You don't look so bad yourself. What's up?"

"What's up?" Spence put his hands on his hips. "Rather, I ask you, what's wrong?"

"Nothing other than my whole world swirling down the toilet."

"Don't tell me that the associate producer still has you bent out of shape. You've scored with half the good-looking gals on the beach. Are you going to tell me a woman you never even kissed has you in this state?"

"Firstly, I've never met anyone like her. Never. Not only did she reject me, but she also stabbed me in the back."

"But you're still in love with her?"

Sonny chugged the remainder of the flask and threw it into the ocean. "Yeah, crazy as it sounds, I'm mad about her. I can't get her out of my mind."

"That's not good."

"Maybe it is. Rather, I think about her than UIP superimposing Johnny Bright's image over mine. Rather, I think of Sammi than my name getting expunged from the credits. I'm not allowed to say a word about it." Sonny threw up his hands. "And I can't do a damn thing about it. Hang Ten may cancel my sponsorship when they find out, and I've already spent the bonus they gave for making the movie and thinking they're getting free advertising."

"Oh, come on, Sonny," Spence touched his shoulder, "You're still the best surfer in Southern California, and maybe even the world, and you surely haven't lost your looks. You'll regain your mojo." Spence smelled the alcohol on Sonny's breath. "But not that way."

"Yeah. Sure. I'm the best surfer." He ran his hand through his hair. "Unfortunately, I've alienated many potential sponsors and pissed off a lot of the judges. Remember that dude, Scott, who wanted to fight me? The judges gave him the Mysticurl Open. They didn't even give me a place."

"Scott? Scott Young a better surfer than you? You've got to be kidding me. I bet everyone knows that you should've won it."

"Yeah, everyone who saw it." Sonny lowered his head, "But not everyone who will only read about it. The sponsors only look at the won, lost ledger." Sonny looked up. He put his hands on his hips. "And don't tell me to get over Sammi. You have Penny. I never told you this, but she's the finest gal

I've ever met. Sammi comes off as unapproachable. It's like she exists on a higher plane. That's not Penny, Spence. She's a real person, living in the real world. She's someone you can talk to, a soulmate. And gorgeous looking, dare I add? As hooked as I am on Sammi's appearance, Penny's looks are just as appealing, just different." Sonny chuckled. "I bet now you're glad I'm hooked on Sammi. Don't worry, buddy, I've known from day one that I'm not Penny's type. I'm saying this so you will appreciate what you got. Sometimes I don't think you see what everyone else sees."

"Now that she's gone, I know you're right. Imagine that." Spence slapped Sonny's arm. "Here I took you for a shallow person, but you read my heart and mind better than a shrink or psychic."

"Did you say, gone?" Sonny blanched.

"Yeah, gone," Spence lowered his head. "She left to stay with her grandparents at their horse ranch in West Virginia."

"West Virginia? If ever I met a true California girl, it's your Penny Williams."

"Penny's story is the same as many Southern California beauties. Her mother won Miss West Virginia. She moved to California, hoping to be a movie star. That never happened, of course. Nevertheless, she met and married a ballplayer with the Hollywood Stars, had children, and settled here."

"Why did she leave? Did you have a fight or something?"

"No," Spence looked away. "Nothing like that, nothing at all."

"Talk to me, man." Sonny moved in front of him. "What's wrong? Why did she leave you?"

"She didn't exactly leave me," Spence took a deep breath. "Unfortunately, I don't think she's coming back." Spence gritted his teeth. "She says she needs time to sort things out." He shook his head. "We both know what that means."

"Yeah, I'm sorry, Spence. You know my history. Before our Associate Producer, Miss Sammi Wray, came along, I dumped them, not vice versa." Sonny grabbed Spence's shoulders. "You've been my best friend for years," Sonny smirked, "I seem like a popular dude, yet you're my only true friend. I also counted Penny as a friend. I got to know her. She would never just up and leave unless something huge happened."

Spence started walking away.

"Spence," Sonny ran up to him. "Talk to me."

"All right," Spence took a deep breath. "I'll tell you. Arthur Feldman."

"Yeah, the officious, tyrannical prick from Beach Party USA." Sonny scratched his head. "Just thinking about that jackass makes me admire Sammi even more." Sonny closed his eyes and pictured her. "She can handle him. No one else can."

"Sonny," Spence inhaled deeply. "He sexually assaulted Penny. Okay. He didn't manage to stick his prick in her, but he violated and tortured her just the same."

"What? Violated? Tortured?"

"Nothing can prepare a man for the horror that I witnessed. Penny bolted from her office wearing nothing but a bikini bottom, screaming for all she's worth, while that revolting lech Feldman chased her with his pants around his ankles." Spence looked at Sonny. He detected that the corners of his lips moved slightly upward. Spence put his hands on his hips. "I get it, Sonny. Yes, we laughed at that clip of British comic Benny Hill chasing a gal with his pants around his ankles to *Yakety Sax*."

"Everyone in America laughed when seeing Benny Hill on the Ed Sullivan Show."

"This is no laughing matter, Sonny. This was more of a gothic horror movie. Unfortunately, it wasn't the British actress, Barbara Steele. It was Penny Williams, the woman I love, running from an unthinkable fate. It may have destroyed her. As it is, the bastard injured her and severely traumatized her. God only knows if she'll ever be the same." Spence lowered his head. "Now here I am left alone, wondering."

"Now we understand why Penny's mother always begged her not to be an actress." Sonny pursed his lips. "What did you do?"

"I picked the bastard up and slammed him. If the floor wasn't concrete, he'd have gone right through it. He's still in the hospital."

"What about the police?"

"Well, it looks like an unwritten agreement. We don't press charges against Feldman for sexual assault, and they don't press charges against me. The witnesses aren't talking."

"I'm glad you gave the bastard what he deserved." Sonny slapped Spence's back.

"Yeah, well, now I know why everyone fears him." Spence pursed his lips. "He has all but barred me from wrestling in California."

"How can he do that?"

"Simple. Universal Entertainment owns United International Pictures. They also own 49.9 percent of the Western Wrestling Alliance. Feldman had them lean on the chief promoter and booker, Simon Beck, to ban me from the territory. They also badmouthed me to other promoters. The candy-ass weasel Beck folded like an umbrella in a hurricane."

"You can go elsewhere, can't you?"

"Al Cohen will take me back in Florida, or maybe Vince McMadden in New York. My old friend Buzz Arlett has some pull with him. Of course, it will mean giving all of this up," he motioned to the ocean, "and going elsewhere will make it even more unlikely that Penny returns to me." Spence shook his head. "In all honesty, my wrestling career has not just stagnated; it's gone backward ever since I had to lose the tag team title five years ago to the Jaguar and the African Lion as a Rustler Brother. I thought every promoter was like Al Cohen, so I returned home to Southern California." Spence pinched his chin. "Now I know otherwise. I also now know I need to find something else to do." He threw up his hands, "I wish I knew what."

"Welcome to the club. All I know is surfing, and it looks like I burned all my bridges behind me." Sonny winced. "I love the sport. Unfortunately, it appears my days making a living at it are over. And speaking of burning, can you smell that campfire up ahead?"

"Yeah, mesquite. Usually, the campfires on this beach are bums burning trash and driftwood."

"No. Not the mesquite," Sonny chuckled. "I smell a little something else."

"Yeah, me too."

"I hate to intrude on a stranger, but I finished my whiskey and threw my flask in the ocean. I think we both need a little escape right now."

"I think we should mind our own business and leave him alone."

"Trust me."

"Where have I heard that before?" Spence smirked.

"No, Spence. I feel a vibe. I feel drawn. I'm sure we'll be welcome."

***

"Spence. Sonny. I've been expecting you." The man added a chunk of mesquite wood to his fire. Sparks fluttered in a circle.

Spence and Sonny looked at each other before returning their gaze to the man. Both figured him in his sixth or seventh decades. The man's muscles were slender and taut like steel cables. His skin looked carved from black alabaster with artistic lines. His narrow nose matched his pointed chin. Gray tipped his dreadlocks. Spence broke the silence, "How did you…"

"Spence Carter, the wrestler, and Sonny Dyer, the Malibu International surfing champion. Both your lives have breached the precipice." He continued to gaze at the flames. "Sit."

Spence and Sonny looked at each other. Spence shrugged. Both sat.

"Look at the ocean. Did you know that it circulates from this shore to the globe's every shore?"

"Yes, sir." Sonny crossed his legs. "It's called the Thermohaline Circulation. I made it a point to learn about the ocean and how waves work. My knowledge of oceanography gives me an edge over my competition. It helps me choose which sea swells will turn into the best surfing wave." Sonny raised his hands. "People think being a professional surfer is only about having fun. The competition is cutthroat. I must prepare the same as an athlete at the highest level of any sport."

"So, you know the ocean is part of many nations." The man lit a ceramic pipe with orange and blue designs. He handed it to Spence.

Spence perused the pipe. "What do I call you?" He smiled and looked at Sonny. "He called you 'Sir.' That's a first. I assure you that everyone else is either 'dude', 'man', or 'bro'."

"Call me Nangolo."

Spence puffed on the pipe. "What is this?" He held up the pipe. "I thought it was reefer. It's something else." Spence closed his eyes and tilted his head back as a wave of euphoria washed over him. "Not that I'm complaining." He snapped his head toward Sonny and then back to Nangolo. He nodded. Spence handed Sonny the pipe.

Sonny took the pipe and inhaled. "The sea is also timeless. Sometimes I ponder the waves and can imagine centuries past." He took another long puff. "Look. I can see Sir Francis Drake's landing party." Sonny took another hit.

'*Sammi, Sammi*', Sonny's image of Sir Francis Drake shifted to Sammi Wray wearing a black bikini with gold fringes. She walked toward him with feline sway, her lips silently articulated, '*Sonny, I love you.*'

"Sir Francis Drake?" Spence shook his head. "You saw Sir Francis Drake while *pondering* the waves? Pondering? That's a switch from *Cowabunga! Surf's up!* This must be some powerful stuff." Spence looked at the pipe, saw white powder mixed with the green leaves, and puffed.

Nangolo dropped another small log on the fire. He waved the sparks into a vortex. "Sonny. Until now, you had never loved. It's not that you're incapable. It just never happened. Now, after all these years, your yearning for love, a need you never perceived or acknowledged, has blossomed into an oasis of trees and flowers, and birds with feathers of every hue and splendor."

"Yes. Her name is Sammi." Sonny closed his eyes and pictured her emerging from behind green fronds with hyacinth and lilac flowers in her brunette tress. "Sammi."

"Yet what she feels for you is like a baron dessert with only lizards and snakes." Nangolo blew on the fire. Sparks dispersed like fireflies. "Her rejection has stung your heart like a scorpion's barb."

A tear welled in the corner of Sonny's eye.

Spence took another hit from the pipe. Nangolo took it and handed it to Sonny. Nangolo opened his hands. "Spence. You found a love denied even to the angels. She is a splendor to the eyes and a salve to the heart. Have you ever reached into the ocean and tried to grab a handful of water?"

"Yes. Often when paddling out into the surf."

"What happened?"

"I can feel the water, its texture, and its temperature, but it slips away, and I am left with nothing."

Nangolo nodded to Spence. "Not only is Penny…"

"How did you know her name?"

Nangolo held up his palm. "That's not important. Not only have you lost Penny, but you lost wrestling."

"Who are you? How do you know these things?" Spence hunched his shoulders. "Why must you remind me?" He took the pipe from Sonny and held it up to Nangolo. "I smoked this stuff with you for an escape, not to face bitter reality. I have plenty of time for that."

"And you, Sonny. Nangolo took the pipe from Spence and handed it to Sonny. "People pretended to like you. They saw you as someone to be seen with. You're handsome and a champion surfer. You were what made a crowd the in crowd. Yet many now take joy in your downfall. As surfing titles fade, so will you. Now that Sammi has broken your heart, your struggle to find the love that can fill your emptiness will elude you. Unless…"

"Just who are you?" Spence stood. "I'm asking again, how the hell do you know these things? Like I said, we have enough problems. The last thing I need is you rubbing it in." Spence's brain whirled. He lost his balance and sat.

"Spence." Sonny rested his arms on his folded knees. "Let's hear him out. Any suggestion at this point is a good one."

"You two are chosen. We had to wait until you were humbled and broken." Nangolo gazed into the fire but not at

Spence or Sonny. "Ultimately, she will choose only one of you."

"She?" Spence shrugged. "I'm too stoned to even move, much less question you. I'm all ears. Talk to us."

"You are both men of the sea. You ride its waves, sometimes you seek harmony, other times conquest. The sea has no boundaries. The planet is its home. There is a place far away. Almost as far as you can point on a map."

"Where?" Sonny took the pipe and took one last puff. "How far away, Nangolo?"

"The most remote Atlantic shore of Africa. In the northern part of what you call South West Africa. The Skeleton Coast. The San people call it "The Land God Made in Anger." Portuguese sailors referred to it as "The Gates of Hell." Here, the surf is too wild for a boat landing. Shipwrecks are scattered in the sands. The Cassimbo fog often shrouds its beaches. The land behind it is miles and miles of arid desert. But the prevailing wind is offshore. What is hell for boats is heaven for surfing."

Sonny closed his eyes. "I wish I had brought my record player. I'd love to hear Debussy's *La Mer* while I listen to you."

"This is getting crazier by the second." Spence pointed at Sonny. "I've known you for how long? I never knew you listened to classical music."

"I keep it secret. If anyone knew, they'd think I'm a square."

Spence shook his head. "Nangolo, I sense you called us here for more than telling us about a secret surfing spot."

"It's more than a surf spot. Its secret stretches beyond what a human mind can fathom. Somewhere along the vast stretches of the Skeleton Coast is the Golden Strand. At a select time, the desert winds erode the surface sand from its mountainous dunes. If the wind is of perfect velocity and direction, it unearths its hidden gold veins and blows billions of gold particles into the surf. Its weight transforms the waves from roiling anger to alluring tranquility. The particles color blue water gold. The breaking white-water sheens like pearls. It's mist flashes rays of rubies, sapphires, topaz, and emeralds."

"It sounds plausible." Spence shrugged. "I imagine it's quite spectacular. But…"

"Spence. Listen to him. I think there's more to it."

"The gold surf breaks in long tubes." Nangolo puffed deeply on the pipe. "It's a surfer's dream to ride one. But only one will be chosen."

"A perfect, tubular wave is rare but not unheard of." Spence raised his hands. "For example, the Pipeline in Hawaii."

"Listen to him closer, Spence. I think it's more than just a ride."

"Once the curl encloses you, you will emerge in Sonoria. It's another world, in another dimension. Part is submerged; part is an island. As it's king, you will rule over both."

"It's king?" Sonny leaned toward Nangolo.

Yes. King Gondor has passed to a realm even farther beyond. Princess Dorabella can't be Queen of Sonoria until she finds a king to reign with her. The mighty Jari Kavumba has chosen one of you to reign with her. Sonny, Princess

Dorabella knows of your devoted, unconditional love for Sammi. Princess Dorabella knows you will love her with even more intensity, and like with Sammi, Dorabella knows it will be from the first second you meet. Spence, Princess Dorabella knows that you loved Penny but failed to show her the appreciation she deserved. Now that you've lost her, Queen Dorabella knows you crave a second chance at love. Sammi's hair is black like a mamba's mouth; Penny's hair is white like a swan's feather. Dorabella's hair is like fine strands of pure gold. Her skin glows like burnished bronze. Sammi's eyes are brown like the Earth, and Penny's eyes are blue as a cloudless sky. Queen Dorabella's eyes shimmer like golden stars and are lusher than a sultan's treasure. Her cheeks and lips are florid as roses, and her teeth shine like polished marble. Her body is firm yet soft with breasts like Charentais. Her love will prove stronger and more ecstatic than any human can love, and she will take you to the delta of nectar where you will want to stay forever. In Sonoria, you can breathe under its crystal waters and surf on its surface. I cannot describe with justice the beauty of Dorabella's palace and the splendor of Sonoria's flora. As for Princess Dorabella, I only attempted to tell of her glories. Only your eyes can behold her beauty. Only your nose can smell her aroma. Only your ears can hear the music of her voice. Her touch and taste are unknown to men. She waits to share it with one of you. I can only speak words. Go now. Jari Kavumba is an angry God and will destroy Sonoria if Dorabella can't find the right king. One of you will fulfill both hers and the mighty Kavumba's expectations. It can only happen if you seek and find the Golden Strand. The one not chosen will still find a great reward." Nangolo closed his eyes and sang a strange, incomprehensible chant.

Sonny and Spence stood and staggered away. After a hundred steps or so, they looked back. Nangolo had vanished. The campfire had extinguished. They said nary a word to one another.

***

Spence rose without his alarm clock. His mind was blank. He rifled through his bureau drawers and stuffed a few necessities in his suitcase before grabbing his surfboard. He heard a knock on his door. *'Who could that be at this hour?'* He opened the door.

Sonny Dyer waited with his suitcase in his right hand and a surfboard under his left arm. "Let's go."

End of Part I

Part II

Chapter 1

Spence and Sonny sat beside each other in their wide, economy-class seats on Pan Am Flight 201. Conducting her pre-flight safety check, the flight attendant's hips swayed to avoid passengers' elbows, feet, and jackets strewn over armrests. Sonny rubbed his Claddagh ring, a gift from his grandfather, before smiling and winking at her. She smiled and nodded back. Suddenly, Sonny pictured her auburn hair turning black and her hazel eyes turning rich brown. *'Sammi. Sammi.'* He shook his head. *'No. No. I'm not turning back.'*

The Boeing 707's takeoff G-Force pressed Spence and Sonny into their seatbacks. During the ascent, the aircraft banked to the West. Sonny leaned over Spence and looked out the window. He got a final look at the surf.

"I see what you see. The surf looks great from up here. There's no turning back now, buddy." Spence nodded. "We're going to find something infinitely better. Besides, I've sold everything I own, including my cherry Chevy Impala SS, and I drained all my bank accounts. I have six months to go on my apartment lease." Spence chuckled. "But I don't think my landlord will ever find me."

Sonny sat back and gripped the armrest. "My Deuce Coupe, savings, and what's left of my trust fund. Gone. My sponsors will expect me to reimburse them. We better find the Golden Strand and Sonoria before they find me, or I'm cooked."

"We better hope the men in white suits and butterfly nets don't jump out of a white panel truck and find us first. Imagine if they knew why we're on this flight." Spence chuckled, "They'd give us a one-way ride to the funny farm.

But what if, Sonny? What if Nangolo was just an illusion from whatever we were smoking?"

"What if?" Sonny raised open palms. "We both smoked it together. We both met him, and we both heard him. We both sensed something deeper than just the mystic ramblings of an eccentric. Let's have no doubt." He shook Spence's hand. "Keep the faith."

"Yes. Of course. After all, what do we have to lose?"

"If we had anything to lose, we already lost it." Sonny laughed.

"The fasten seatbelt sign is off." Spence beamed. "Hey, here comes our friend."

The flight attendant's Pan Am uniform hugged her figure as she pushed her cart toward Spence and Sonny's seats.

"Hi, Sammi." Spence imbibed her hyacinth perfume and looked into her eyes. "What do you have in beer?"

"Sammi?" She laughed. "My name is Deloris." She pinched her nametag.

"I'm sorry. I was thinking…"

"It's perfectly okay." Deloris chuckled. "People have called me worse. I'm sure mistaking me for this Sammi is a compliment?"

"The highest." Sonny averted her gaze, tilted his head downward, and briefly smiled.

"As for beer, I've got Budweiser, Schlitz, and Schaffer."

"Hit or an error." Spence chimed in.

Deloris raised her eyebrows, tilted her head, and shrugged.

"I'm a Dodgers fan." Spence leaned toward her. "That reference is from the other Dodgers. You know? When they were the Brooklyn Dodgers. Schaffer Beer sponsored the Ebbets Field scoreboard. The 'h' lit up to indicate if a batter got a hit and the 'e' if it's an error."

"I learn something new every day." Deloris smiled. "I hope this is a hit for you." She opened a can of Schaffer beer and poured Spence a cup. "As for you," she tapped Sonny's hand, "just so you don't commit another error saying my name, you can call me what my friends call me. Dora."

Spence and Sonny looked at each other, nodded, and smiled.

She poured Sonny a cup of Schafer Beer. "What would you two like for dinner? You can choose roast duck with wild rice or sirloin steak with potato gratin."

"The steak." Spence sipped his beer. "Medium rare."

"I like mine medium rare as well. But you better not cook mine at all." Sonny grinned at Dora. "Because you have so much sizzle that it might come burnt to a crisp."

"I'll add some corn to it." She chuckled. "I've heard that one before. Don't worry," she touched his shoulder. "I already like you, so you won't have to find a better line. On the flip side, I may make your steak sizzle, but I can keep your beer cold."

Sonny watched her walk away. '*Hmm…nice…*' He then scanned upward, *the same length as hers but auburn.*'

Spence poked Sonny in the ribs. "I see we're getting the real Sonny Dyer back." He chuckled. "Only you can hit a girl with such a hokey line but get her to like you anyway."

"Not every girl." An image of Sammi popped back into his head. "Dorabella." Sonny closed his eyes and mumbled. "I know you're real. Even if you're not, looking for you will be worth it."

Spence closed his eyes and stretched his legs. He pictured Penny. 'So far away. So far, far away. I never appreciated you, and I let you go. Now I'm pursuing a myth.' He pounded on the seat rest. 'I'd better find the Golden Strand and the portal to Sonoria. Princess Dorabella, I hope you're real and you're everything the wise man said about you.'

***

After five hours, the plane descended to New York's Idlewild airport. Spence caught a glimpse of the Manhattan skyline. *I wish we had made time to stay.* Spence pressed his nose to the window.

Sonny tilted his head back and closed his eyes. 'Sammi drove me to seek you, Dorabella. Dora sure is a step in the right direction. Why do I want the unattainable? Better perk up your confidence, Sonny. 'Nangolo said Dorabella will only choose one.' He glanced at Spence. 'It won't be me until I get over myself.'

After the plane landed and stopped taxiing, Spence and Sonny walked toward the exit door. Deloris stood by the door to bid the passengers farewell. "Goodbye, Spence. Goodbye, Sonny. I hope that I can serve you on your return flight."

"That's if we return." Spence nodded. "Our next flight is to London and then Johannesburg, South Africa. We then plan on trekking overland to the coast of South West Africa."

"Oh my. I will say a prayer for you boys." Deloris took both of Sonny's hands. "Best of luck. BOAC, British Overseas Airways Corporation, flies out of Terminal C. You had better take the shuttle. Walking would take too long. You don't want to risk missing your flight."

Sonny pecked Deloris's cheek.

She smiled.

He imbibed her hyacinth perfume before walking on and not looking back.

***

While departing BA099 at London's Heathrow Airport, Sonny blocked Sammi from his thoughts, imagined Dorabella, and sang to himself Nat King Cole's '*Around the World.*'

"You better stop singing and stick to surfing, or the next fight you need to get bailed out of might be with me." Spence laughed. "A better Nat King Cole song for us to sing is '*A Nightingale Sang in Berkeley Square*', after all, we're in London. Let's find it in a record store. Leave the singing to Nat King Cole."

"This is my first time all the way across an ocean. Hang Ten sent me to Hawaii for the Makaha International Surfing Championship, but that was only halfway across the ocean, and I was still in the United States."

"Don't worry about a thing. I wrestled here for three months. We've got 26 hours until our flight to Johannesburg; I'll be your tour guide."

"Did you wrestle as a heel?"

"Yeah, I did the Biff Rustler schtick. It went over too well. The stereotype is that every Brit is polite and sedate," Spence snickered and shook his head. "That's not their wrestling fans. London has rough neighborhoods and plenty of people you don't want to face in a scrap." Spence grinned. "I got plenty of bumps and bruises to prove it."

***

"This place looks inviting." Sonny pointed at an artsy wooden sign hanging over dual heavy oak doors with polished brass fittings. "The King's Arms." He pinched his chin.

"Here we cross the North American continent and the Atlantic Ocean to a city of culture, history, and museums, yet we end up in a bar. Spence chuckled. "I don't remember Nangolo saying anything about finding Sonoria and Dorabella in a pub." Spence smiled at Sonny. "But a cold beer and a hot meal are the next best things. And who knows? Maybe Bennie Hill or Barbara Steele will walk in. We need a good laugh, and Barbara Steele will make you forget about Sammi."

"If she doesn't kill me first."

"It's only in the movies." Spence held Sonny's arm. "Come on, I'm buying the first round."

The King's Arms pub boasted stained glass windows depicting medieval knights, damsels, and horses. The sunset glowed on the windows.

"Speaking of hot, I've already had enough of this cold, dank weather." Sonny rubbed his hands together. "Let's sit by the fireplace." Sonny and Spence sat in wooden, leather-backed chairs at a table under one of the pub's thick ceiling beams.

A stocky waitress wearing a Victory Badge honoring her fallen father from World War II ambled over. "Fancy a pint and a hot meal, love."

"I'd love a pint and a *hawt* meal."

The round-faced waitress with a Mo Howard bowl cut chuckled at Sonny's attempt at a British accent. "You Yanks need to realize that we speak the proper English. Call me Isabella."

Spence and Sonny looked at one another. They nodded and smiled.

"By the looks of your tans, you're not used to our nippy weather. Our shepherd's pie will perk your nithered bones."

"Sounds great." Sonny looked over at the beer pumps. "I'll have a Lucky Lager."

"You better leave Lucky Lager back across the pond." Isabella laughed. "You boys look like you need a Guinness Stout."

"Sounds like a plan." Sonny pointed upwards. "But you forgot something?"

"What might that be, love?" Isabella crossed her arms.

"Never mind." Sonny beamed. "Love." He chuckled. "You just remembered."

"You Yanks are worse than the Italians and French." Isabella guffawed. "Love."

"I apologize for him." Spence folded his arms.

"Apologize?" Isabella beamed. "Englishmen never flirt with us plump birds. At least not when sober. I appreciate compliments from anyone, including Italians, Frenchmen, and especially this Yankee." Isabella placed her hand on Sonny's shoulder.

***

Spence and Sonny were on the final sip of their third pint of Guinness Stout. "Keep your eyes straight ahead." Sonny finished his beer. "Two men at the bar are looking you over. They look tough. I don't want any trouble."

Spence glanced at two tough-looking men wearing denim jackets and steel-toed work boots. The larger of the two had his hair cut to bristles and was staring at him. Spence turned away after brief eye contact.

"Uh oh, don't look now, Spence. He's coming over. I'm the lover. You're the fighter. I hope you're ready."

"Now I know who you are!" The man extended his hand. "It took some time. After all, you cut and washed the dye from your hair, and you dropped some weight, but I recognized the face, and your voice gave you away. Biff Rustler."

Spence looked at him for two seconds before shaking his hand.

"I'm Ian. He's my mate, Gavin." He pointed to his friend, who now stood. Although more compact, Gavin was more muscular than Ian. "Hey, Isabella, get these blokes two pints. Put 'em on my slate."

"You got me." Spence chuckled, "Only I was Biff Rustler. Now I'm Spence Carter."

"At first, I couldn't stand the sight of ya, and my girlfriend hated you more. What did you expect? A big, brash, loud-mouthed cowboy disrespecting us? But after my bird and me called it a day, I had to like you because she still hated you." Ian guffawed. "Mind if we join you?"

"Seeing how you bought us a round," Spence held open hands toward the two empty seats, "by all means."

Isabella put four-pint glasses of Guinness Stout on the table.

"What brings you to our shores?" Gavin sipped his beer. "You stayin' to grapple?"

"No. As of right now, I'm outta the business. My friend Sonny and I are headed to Johannesburg, South Africa, in the morning. After we land, we're trekking cross country to South West Africa, call it like the Beach Boys' song, a 'Surfin Safari'."

A young man, Spence's height but with Sonny's trim physique, stood and walked over to their table. "Did I hear you're headed for South Africa and are looking for surf? I'm from Durban, South Africa. If you don't mind sharks, Durban's got some boss waves." He paused and stared at Sonny. "Now I know you! You're Sonny Dyer! I've seen your picture in the surfing mags." He shouted to his wife. "Hey, Michaila, come over here. It's the American surfing champion, Sonny Dyer."

Michaila walked over. Spence saw that she was a striking blonde. He fell into a trance. *I'm so sorry, Penny. I'll never forget you.*

"I'm Michael, this is my wife, Michaila."

"M and M. Like Mantle and Maris." Spence laughed.

The statuesque woman's complexion contrasted with her husband's. She smiled and nodded.

"Well, Michael, Michaila, pull up a chair and join us." Sonny stood. "We'll make it a party." He chuckled, "You get to buy the first round of six."

Michael pulled a face before holding up five fingers and a thumb to Isabella.

Sonny and Michael tapped glasses. "Michael, tell me about the Skeleton Coast, on the other side of your continent. What's the surf like?"

"I've never been over there. Few people have. You will have to cross the Kalahari and Namib deserts. But I hear it's got lekker surf. The prevailing winds blow offshore, and you will have it all to yourself."

"Do I have to worry about Mr. and Mrs. Shark?"

"The Benguela current runs up the Atlantic coast from Antarctica. It's too cold for tiger sharks and zambies. You only need worry about the blue pointers. But the current brings in lots of fish, so they're well fed. You'll have to wear a wetsuit, of course. Just hope they don't mistake you for a seal." Michael snickered. "The Durban, Indian Ocean coast, gets the warm Mozambique current. It brings warm water sharks like zambies and tigers, but is cool enough for blue pointers. Otherwise saying, warm enough to bring 'em. Cool enough to keep 'em active."

"What are blue pointers and zambies?" Spence shrugged his shoulders.

"Oh, come on, Spence," Sonny smirked. "You've met enough foreign surfers in California to know that South

Africans call bull sharks Zambezi sharks and great white sharks, blue pointers."

"The Loch Ness has no surf, so you don't have to mind our monsters." Ian laughed. "I reckon if we're going to drink to sharks and monsters, we need something stronger." He stood and gestured. "Isabella, six shots a Jameson, no, we got Yanks, make it Jack Daniels, and six more pints of Guinness."

"Anything else?" Isabella lowered her tray to her side.

"Yeah, make it seven. Join us, why don't you?"

Isabella balanced her tray of thirteen drinks on her fingertips, sauntered over, and placed them before her customers as fast as a casino dealer would cards.

Ian held his shot glass aloft. "To sharks and monsters. Let this douse anything else eating us."

The seven downed their shots. Everyone but Isabella chased with beer. Michaila spotted Isabella sweating and patting her stomach. She gave Isabella her beer. Isabella gulped and wiped her brow. "Thanks, Micki, you're a true lady."

Gavin chugged his entire beer. "I know why these two Yanks are here. What brings you Springboks to our shore?"

"My mother lives here. I'm visiting her." Michael turned to Spence and Sonny. "My father is American. He and my mother split. He lives across the pond. That may be our next stop. Where can I find some big waves in America?"

"Hawaii is now part of America, but I know you mean the continental United States. I'm from Southern California." Sonny finished his beer. "But if you're looking for big surf, and I mean scary big, go north, up the Pacific

Coast Highway. Twenty-five miles south of 'Frisco, you'll find a spot called Mavericks. But it ain't for greenies. It's big and it's gnarly."

"I'm no greenie, and our shores are plenty deadly." Michael crossed his arms. "I'm no moffie. I'm gonna scope out Mavericks first thing."

"It's not about you bein' the big man." Michaila grabbed Michael's arm. "It's about common sense." She shook her head. "When it comes to surfing, if anyone knows what he's talking about, it's Sonny Dyer. I don't mind you being young and dumb. Just stick around with me to grow old and smart."

"All right. But I do want to scope it out." Michael pinched his short-cropped beard. "Sonny Dyer here's good at something else."

"What's that?"

"Drinking for free." Michael laughed.

"All right," Sonny smirked. "I get it." He stood and pointed. "Isabella, another round of Jack and Stout for everyone, including you."

"Coming right up, love."

"Hey, you never call us love." Ian tilted his head.

"That's so I don't break your heart." Isabella turned and walked toward the bar. Gavin, Michael, Mikaila, Spence, and Sonny laughed at him. Ian blushed.

***

"I'll make a deal with you all." Isabella served the party their shots and brews. "Sing along with me, and I'll make it an early happy hour. Two rounds for the price of one."

"The next one's my turn," Ian smirked, "So, I guess I don't gotta pay."

"Not only are you gonna pay." Isabella laughed. "You're also going to be the first to sing. All together now, "They'll be bluebirds over, the white cliffs of Dover, tomorrow, just you wait and see." Isabella waved her arms. The pub sang with her, "I'll never forget the people I met. Braving those angry skies. I remember well as the shadows fell, the light of hope in their eyes. And though I'm far away. I still hear them say, bombs up. But when the dawn comes, they'll be bluebirds over the white cliffs of Dover, tomorrow, just you wait and see."

"I thought you said I had to sing first?" Ian grinned. "I'm a longshoreman by trade. Sometimes my work takes me to Liverpool. The other week, I went to the pub and heard a local act. They're gettin' popular. You may've heard of 'em. Sing along with me." Ian sang, "She loves you yeah, yeah, yeah." The pub joined him. "She loves you yeah, yeah, yeah; she loves you yeah, yeah, yeah." Ian sang solo, "You think you've lost your love? Well, I saw her yesterday. It's you she's thinking of, and she told me what to say. She says loves you, and you know that can't be bad. Yes, she loves you, and you know you should be glad." The pub sang, "She loves you yeah, yeah, yeah; she loves you yeah, yeah, yeah; she loves you yeah, yeah, yeah."

"Hey, great song, Ian." Spence gulped some beer. "I bet someday it will take America by storm." Spence finished his beer.

"You think so, Spence?" Sonny laughed. "How much do you want to bet?" Sonny turned to Ian. "I liked your song. I'm afraid, I can't imagine it getting popular in America."

"Well, it was fun to sing." Spence turned to Michael, "I've got a question for you."

"Ask away, bloke."

"We were told about a place on South West Africa's Skeleton Coast called The Golden Strand."

"Yeah, here in the UK and parts of South Africa, especially among the Boers, they call beaches a strand."

"Michael, I heard of a mysterious beach, strand, along the Skeleton Coast, where, if the berg wind blows just right, it erodes gold particles from the escarpment and disperses them into the surf. Its weight makes a perfect curl and colors the water gold. Even the spray becomes a prism of pearlescent colors."

"Wow! Sounds romantic." Michaila folded her hands. "It's possible. After all, we often nickname the city where you're headed to 'The Reef. That's because Joburg sits on a gold reef." She opened her hands. "So, this Golden Strand? It is possible."

Sonny looked at Spence. Spence looked back and nodded.

"Well, it looks like Isabella wants to close the place and go home." Ian picked up his pint of beer. "One last toast. To the Golden Strand. I hope you find it." The six tapped glasses and stood.

"Isabella, love, I know you want to go home. Bring us one last round." Sonny put his hand over his heart. "It will be on me. Please?"

"How can I say no to my Yankee Prince Charming?"

Isabella carried over a tray with six pint glasses of Guinness. Sonny took a pint from her tray and held it aloft. He sang, "Heda! Heda! Hedo!

"What music are you butchering?" Spence took his beer from Isabella's tray.

"It's from Wagner's Das Rheingold. I'm Donner, God of Thunder, summoning the Gods to Valhalla."

"Wagner?" Michael pulled his face.

"Yes! Wagner! Heda! Heda, Hedo!" Sonny again held his glass aloft. "Heda! Heda, Hedo!" Sonny played the orchestral music in his head while he chugged his entire beer. He suddenly felt a swirling, twirling sensation. He faced Isabella. Her short bowl cut turned into a flowing, over-the-shoulder raven tress. Her eyes grew and shone a lustrous brown. Her plump face turned into a contoured oval. He curled his upper lip to his nostrils. '*Hyacinth*'. "I love you." After staggering six steps, he fell into her arms.

She held him up. "I love you, too, Sonny, but you gotta go, it's closing time."

Spence walked over, braced his arm around Sonny's waist, and looked at Isabella. "I'll help you with him. Don't worry. We're not driving."

"I've seen worse." Isabella chuckled. "Much worse. I'll call you a hack."

"Thanks. Tell the driver to take us to Heathrow. If we sleep this off in a hotel, we're liable to miss our flight." Spence reached into his pocket. "Here's an American custom I think you'll like." He handed her a twenty-pound note. "Keep the change."

Isabella's hazel eyes lit up as she held the twenty-pound note.

"Come on, Sonny, help me say goodbye to our new friends. We gotta go now."

"Leb Wohl. Leb Wohl." Sonny sang.

"I don't know how such a lousy singer comes up with that stuff." Spence continued to hold Sonny up. "But you're proving a world of mystery. Maybe it's you that Dorabella will choose to rule her mystery world."

Isabella, Michael, Michaila, Ian, and Andrew sang Spence and Sonny a popular Irving King ditty, "Show me the way to go home, I'm tired and I want to go to bed. I had a little drink about an hour ago, and it's gone straight to my head."

Chapter 2

"Carlton Hotel." Spence and Sonny strapped their surfboards to the roof of a waiting taxi at Johannesburg, South Africa's Jan Smuts airport.

"Yebo." The driver disembarked and pulled on the straps securing the surfboard. He then alighted from his taxi and drove on the M2 highway toward downtown Johannesburg.

"This isn't what I **expected**." Sonny rode in the front seat and turned to the driver. "All I see is modern highways, cars, and skyscrapers. Where are the elephants, giraffes, and lions?"

"Give me a couple hundred bucks and pay for my gas." The driver's lean black arm bulged as he steered around a curve. "And I take you. Don't worry. The Carlton Hotel is the real Africa. It's made of mud and has a thatched roof." The driver laughed. "I know the manager. Slip me an extra twenty and I'll make sure you can use the indoor toilet. Not that there's anything wrong with the outdoor toilet. The cobras like it. But you'll have to bathe in a stream. Beware. It has crocodiles."

Sonny gasped.

"As a reward for successfully pulling my friend's leg," Spence laughed. "I'll tip you a twenty above the meter. He's Sonny; I'm Spence."

"I'm Sipho."

"Hey, Sipho, you impress me as knowing Johannesburg better than anyone. After you drop us off, keep the meter running, we'll be right back after we check in and secure our luggage and surfboards. Can you take us to an honest auto dealership that sells Land Rovers?"

"Yebo." He kept both hands on the steering wheel while glancing back at Spence, "I can take you to a dealer selling many Land Rovers." He laughed. "I can't promise he'll be honest."

***

"Sipho was right about the selection." Spence walked through the car lot."

"We both know our cars," Sonny brushed his hand over a gray 1962 Land Rover 11A. "But let me do the talking. After all, you can't bullshit a bullshitter."

"Can I help you two?" A man wearing brown shoes and white socks approached them. He wore a short pants khaki safari suit; his gut put a lump in its short-sleeved jacket-like top.

Spence and Sonny looked at each other. Sonny extended his hand. "Sonny Dyer."

"Ah, a Yankee accent." The sales manager shook hands with him. "What part of America are you boys from?"

"California." Sonny smiled. "The same as my partner in crime, Spence."

Spence shook hands with the sales manager.

"I'm Trevor Botha. I take it you're here to buy a Land Rover."

"If you can give us an honest deal, yes." Sonny put his right foot forward.

"I'll make like your first president and not tell a lie," Trevor chuckled. "What do you need it for?"

100

"We're driving across your country to South West Africa's Skeleton Coast." Spence nodded. "The Beach Boys record says it all, we're on a Surfin' Safari."

"Is surf all you're looking for on the Skeleton Coast?" Trevor scratched his temple. "Durban has excellent surf, first-class resort hotels, and it's only a six-hour drive."

"The Skeleton Coast calls us." Sonny stepped forward. "We need a vehicle to make it possible."

"That I can help you with." Trevor crossed his arms. "Even if all you'll find on the Skeleton Coast is driftwood, shipwrecks, and big surf."

"There's far more to it. And you'd think us crazy if we told you everything."

"And if you think we're daft," Spence laughed, "you may think you can fleece us."

"Daft? Fleece? I can tell you went through London to get here. You learn fast. You'll do well in my country. Don't worry. I already think you're crazy for wanting to drive to the West Coast. But if you're looking for something on the Skeleton Coast, you may find it." Trevor held up open hands. "After all, hardly anyone has ever been there to find it first." Trevor nodded. "You don't have to tell me what you're looking for on the Skeleton Coast. Over there," Trevor motioned with his arms, "I have exactly what you're looking for. It will get you to the Skeleton Coast and handle its beaches once you're there."

Spence and Sonny followed Trevor across his lot.

"What do you think, boys?" Trevor rubbed his hand on the hood of a pastel green vehicle. It had flat aluminum body panels with exposed rivets and rounded shoulder lines. "This is a 1962 Series 11A. You won't find better than this."

"Does it have the 2.25-liter inline-four petrol engine or the 2.0-liter Diesel?" Spence sharpened his eyes.

"It's the standard 2.25-liter petrol. The Diesel option gets better fuel economy. Nevertheless, the issue is availability. When driving across a barren desert, you won't find many petrol garages. If you find one but it doesn't sell Diesel, Jy is vrek sleg af."

"I don't speak that language," Spence chuckled, "but I get the meaning. We'll take the petrol-fueled one. We also need four-wheel drive."

"All Series 11A Land Rovers have four-wheel drive."

"And I see it has a long 109-inch wheelbase." Sonny looked down at its rear tires.

"Yes, it does. It doesn't look like I can pull one over on you." Trevor placed his hand on the Land Rover. "You know your vehicles." Trevor chuckled. "This one has an important option for your needs." Trever brushed his hand over its roof. "It has the optional tropical roof. It's double-layered for better ventilation."

"Your weather doesn't feel tropical. It feels like Southern California's but with thinner air." Spence smiled. "I like it."

"Johannesburg is even higher than your city of Denver. Even though we're North of the Tropic of Capricorn, our elevation gives us mild weather. Once you drive down from the highveld and reach the Kalahari and Namib deserts, you'll think you're in California's Mojave Desert and Death Valley."

“You know a lot about the United States.”

“I sell Land Rovers. Many of my buyers are foreigners. Much of my business is with safari tour companies. A successful businessman learns about his customers. Most of my foreign customers buy one for an animal safari. You boys are the first going on a Surfin’ Safari.” Trevor grinned. “I’ve never driven across two countries and two deserts, but I will include what you need. Buy now and I’ll throw in four 50-liter containers free of charge. For a trek of the magnitude you are planning, you had better fill two with additional petrol and two with drinking and radiator water. Moreover, stop at every petrol garage and fill up, regardless of your current need. Don’t take any unnecessary chances. You will never know how far away the next petrol garage is. Trust me.” Trevor opened his hands.

“Trust you?” Sonny laughed. “In California, trust me means, screw you.”

“I can’t pull one over on you mechanically.” Trevor chuckled. “I can exaggerate my shipping and import costs, but I won’t do that to you. Come to my office. I’ll show you the documentation.”

Spence and Sonny nodded to each other.

“Will you be paying in South African Rand or US dollars?”

Chapter 3

"This Kalahari Desert is far from barren." Sonny gazed across the landscape. "It reminds me of the Chihuahuan Desert of Texas and New Mexico."

"Yeah, but nobody driving down Interstate 10 is on the lookout for Elephants, Rhinos, or lions."

"Unless they smoked that stuff Nangolo shared with us."

"Let's not lose faith now, Sonny. We're not exactly at the last exit to Brooklyn. Our last chance to turn around was 10,000 miles ago. I don't know what we'll find in Henties Bay, but we've already traveled halfway around the world and still haven't arrived."

"Ain't that the truth? We just arrived in the Kalahari Desert, and we still must cross the Namib Desert. Remember, Trevor warned us it was a giant Death Valley. "Hey, look!" Sonny sat up and pointed. "A rhino! Let's try out this thing's four-wheel drive and go over for a closer look."

"I don't think that's a good idea." Spence stopped along the road. "That Rhino looks like a tank with a horn."

"Come on, Spence." Sonny grabbed Spence's shirt sleeve. "We're in Africa. There's more adventure here than just surf."

"We're here to find the Golden Strand, Sonoria, and Princess Dorabella, not get gored by a rhino."

"He's not going to attack us. Besides, even if he charges, our Land Rover can outrun him."

"Oh, what the heck. Maybe you're right, Sonny. After all, we are in Africa and crossed three continents and an ocean to get here." Spence jerked the wheel to the right. Their Land Rover bounced over the unsettled terrain.

"Wow!" Sonny pointed at the rhinoceros. "He looks bigger than anything I've seen in a zoo."

The Rhinoceros snorted.

"I don't like the way he's looking at us." Spence shook his head.

"Relax, Bro, rhinos have terrible eyesight. He can hardly see us. Turn off the ignition so the engine noise won't bother him."

"I don't like that idea." Spence turned off the ignition. "But fewer things to bother him, the better."

The Rhinoceros snorted twice. He walked four steps toward the Land Rover, lowered his head, and snorted again.

"I don't like this…Oh, shit!"

The rhinoceros lowered his head, put his horn forward, and charged the Land Rover.

Spence turned the ignition. An electronic grind. "No! No! No!" He closed his eyes, tilted his head skyward, and silently moved his lips. He turned the key again. "Come on!" *Grind.* "Come on!" *Grind.* "Come on!"

The ground rumbled as the Rhinoceros galloped closer.

"Yes!" The Land Rover turned over.

"Get us out of here!" Sonny covered his eyes. "Please, God!"

The Land Rover's wheels spun in the desert sand. The Rhino was close enough for Spence to look into his beady eyes. He leaned forward on the steering wheel as the Land Rover's tires gripped the sand. The Rhinoceros ran faster than the Land Rover could move through the desert. He lowered his horn to gore the Land Rover and flip it over. A screeching noise and the scent of burning rubber marked the Land Rover reaching the road. The Rhinoceros chased the Land Rover for a few pregnant seconds before stopping and returning to the veld. He grazed on Kalahari sand grass as if never disturbed.

Spence sped down the road.

"You can slow down now." Sonny uncovered his eyes. "He's gone. Thank God!"

"You thank God. I'll thank me," Spence backfisted Sonny, "You idiot! 'Go off-road for a closer look? Turn off the ignition so the noise won't bother him?" Spence shoved Sonny. "If we don't find the Golden Strand, Sonoria, and Princess Dorabella, you're to blame." Spence prodded. "You never had any sense. First, a rhino damn near kills me because of your advice. Now we're alone in a godforsaken desert somewhere in Africa, all because you convinced me to listen to some dope-smoking bum. If not for me, you'd have gotten your ass kicked a hundred times over." Spence pursed his lips and looked down the road. "Only God knows what further trouble you'll get us in."

Sonny massaged his mouth to relieve the punch's physical pain. A tear dripped from his left eye.

***

"It looks like a border crossing of sorts." Sonny took one hand off the steering wheel and pointed at a lowered orange and white boom gate.

"You better slow down and stop."

A stocky, white border guard in short pants, a khaki uniform top, and a lightweight pith helmet held up an arm-extended halt gesture. Two smaller black border guards wore the same uniform.

"Can I help you?" Sonny kept two hands on the wheel and smiled.

"May I see your passports?" The white border guard walked over to the Land Rover driver's side.

"Sure thing, sir." Spence leaned over Sonny, shuffled through the dash tray, and found their passports. He handed them to the official.

"American, I see." The border guard perused their passports. "You came a long way. Why are you here?"

"We're on a Surfin' Safari," Sonny beamed.

"Well, you can turn back in the direction you came from. Drive about 2,000 kilometers. You'll reach Durban. You'll find plenty of surf there. Or you can head 2,000 kilometers south. Cape Town also has plenty of Ocean. But I'm not letting you into this country. You don't have a visa."

Sonny and Spence blanched. "What do you mean, officer?" Sonny pointed to the passport. "Our visa is right there."

"That visa is for South Africa," the border guard laughed. "This is the entrance to South West Africa."

"Isn't it that different parts of the same country?"

"You didn't do your homework," the guard smirked. "South Africa administers South West Africa under a League of Nations mandate; to enter South West Africa, you need a visa and permission from the South African government. You don't have the required paperwork for my country. I'm sorry you had to learn the hard way. Now turn around and go to Durban or Cape Town. Get your passports stamped while there and come back."

"But he's a World-class professional surfer." Spence saw the guard furrow the brow of his wrinkled face. "The name Sonny Dyer is famous on the international surfing circuit. He plans on writing about your Skeleton Coast in international publications. He can give your country the notoriety it deserves. That means tourist money."

"I couldn't care less about surfing." He put his hands on his hips. "Besides, most of you surfers are broke kids. I see camping gear in your truck. How does a bunch of kids on a budget help our economy?"

Sonny pointed at Spence. "He's the World champion professional wrestler."

The border guard pinched his chin. "I can see that by your physique."

"Yes. And he is here to give the South African champion, Jan Wilkens, a world title bout. But Mr. Wilkens wants the fight outside of South Africa." Sonny rested a hand on the steering wheel and the other forearm on the door frame. He smiled at the officer. "We're negotiating a title fight for your country. First, we are checking out Windhoek's South West Stadium to see how we can fix it up for a world title fight.""Why didn't you say so?" the border guard beamed. "Jan Wilkens is a hero in our part of the world. We can only read about him or see him in movie newsreels. Many in my country would kill to see him in a title fight. I'll tell you what." The border guard smiled. "When you get to Windhoek, check in at the Tintenpalast. I'll call ahead. There you can get your visa processed. If you promise to do that, I will pass you through."

"Yes, Sir!" Sonny tapped his fingers across his chest. "Cross my heart and hope to die."

The border guard nodded to the two black border guards. They lifted the boom gate.

"Sonny, now I know why I chose you to be my little brother." Spence leaned over and kissed Sonny's cheek. "You were brilliant. Absolutely brilliant. And how on Earth do you know about Jan Wilkens? After all, I'm a professional wrestler and I've never heard of him."

"When we were in Trevor Botha's office doing the paperwork on the Land Rover." Sonny winked. "I saw a framed, autographed photo of Jan Wilkens on his wall."

Chapter 4

"We made it." Spence raised his arms and shook his fists. "Henties Bay! By my calculations, we've traveled 12,000 miles."

"Sometimes I think the final leg should've been in the back of a white panel truck." Sonny kept both hands on the wheel. "Our driver would be wearing a clean white coat."

"Here I thought I was the straight man and you the joker. Come on, Sonny, how many people in the know have we spoken to? All of them say the Golden Strand is plausible. Let's not doubt now."

"All things considered, it's already a minor miracle we've gotten this far." Sonny grimaced. "Let's not forget our lives took a nosedive back in California. We still have no idea who Nangolo is, where he came from, and where he went."

"You better help me find Sonoria, because you and that rhino almost sent me to a different promised land."

"I'll take the rhino horn over your fist to the mouth."

"You made up for it with fast thinking at the border crossing." Spence kissed Sonny's cheek. "I hope that makes it feel better."

"I sure hope you meet Princess Dorabella soon." Sonny rubbed his cheek. "I'm starting to worry about you."

"What if she chooses you?" Spence laughed and squeezed Sonny's hand. "Nangolo said only one of us can reign with her as king."

"Nangolo said the one she doesn't choose will also find a great reward. I hope she chooses me." Sonny smirked and pulled his hand away. "At least I know if I'm in Sonoria, I'm not your reward." He chuckled. "I forget. Is she Princess Dorabella or Queen Dorabella?"

"We got blitzkrieg stoned smoking whatever Nangolo was smoking. What I remember is him saying Dorabella is a princess. Her father, the King of Sonoria, recently died. But she can't be queen until she finds a husband to reign as king and queen."

"And that's why we're here." Spence pointed at the buildings along the street. "Except for the Dutch facades, this could be an American village. It's not too big, but it's got everything we need and more. You see, Sonny, I read that the guy who discovered this town, Major Hendrik "Henty" Stefanus van der Merve, made it a tourist destination from the start."

"Yeah, we talked about that." Sonny looked forward. "It's mostly for sport fishermen; we're among the first surfers."

"Fishermen come here because the Benguela current is rich with fish. It's a cold-water current. That means just one thing. Great White Sharks. I hope the only thing on their menu is fish and seals."

"Our black wetsuits will make us look like a seal." Sonny grinned. "At least it doesn't make us taste like a seal."

"Let's hope they never take a free sample." Spence pointed. "Hey! The De Duine Hotel. This is it, my friend. 12,000 miles. We've made it."

***

Spence and Sonny entered their De Duine Hotel room. Sonny dropped his luggage at the foot of his bed and leaned his surfboard in the corner. "Fancy name and exotic location for this hotel, but this room belongs in a monastery or Spartan army barracks."

"Yeah," Sonny placed his luggage on his bed. "It doesn't even have a TV. Even some of the inmates at San Quentin have TVs."

"Breaking news, Sonny. South Africa and South West Africa don't yet have television." Spence started unbuttoning his shirt. "We're here to find the Golden Strand, not vacation."

"If a vacation is getting away from it all," Sonny chuckled, "this place is ideal."

Spence tossed his shirt onto his bed."I didn't see a gym here either." Sonny pointed at Spence's torso. "How are you going to keep that up? You don't look that way from pretzels and beer."

"I no longer have to worry about wrestling." Spence glanced in a mirror placed on top of a chest of drawers. "I miss pushing heavy weights with Rick. But if I reach our ultimate destination, Sonoria, it won't matter." Sonny sat on the bed. "You're not having doubts, are you?"

"It's only natural to have second thoughts." Sonny reached into his bags for a pair of sunglasses. "Don't worry, Spence. I'm all in."

"Our search begins tomorrow." Spence lay on his bed. "I'm beat. I'm going to rest up. First thing in the morning, we start exploring the Skeleton Coast."

"I'm tired too." Sonny walked toward the door. "But not tired enough to sleep through your snoring. I'm going to walk through town. Maybe try a local beer."

"Suit yourself." Spence threw his shirt at Sonny.

***

Downtown Henties Bay had a row of businesses on each side of its main street, Jakkalsputz Road. Houses of various shapes, sizes, and social classes were scattered in the nearby countryside. At the end of Jakkalsputz Road sat a Cape Dutch-style church. Its gables and walls were whitewashed. Its spire made it the tallest building in town. Sonny stood and stared at the church. *'Why do I feel the urge to go inside?' I'm not religious.'* Sonny walked around its grounds, stopping to admire a stained-glass window. He next walked to the main entrance and pulled on the door. *'Unlocked.'* He skulked through the church's foyer but stopped at the beginning of the sanctuary aisle. Dressed in white, the slender woman leaned over and lit candles in ornate holders by the chancel. *'Her movements, ghostly but alluring'.* Sonny walked closer. *'What gorgeous white hair, white enough to damn near glow in the dark, and what a unique pointed chin. Her skin is so pale, but it makes her florid cheeks stand out, and those lips, glowing, and soft, oh so soft, like Carnelian gems.'*

"Good afternoon." She stood and turned to Sonny.

'Her eyes! They're a shade of baby blue.' "Um, Hi." He looked away from her eyes and leaned backward.

"You speak with an accent. I've heard Americans speak in movies and on the radio. You sound like one."

"Um…Yes…America…Um…I'm an American." Sonny straightened his posture. "Your voice is gorgeous. I love your accent. I can't tell anyone this, but I like opera. Hearing you speak is like listening to Maria Callas sing."

"Thank you," She lowered her head and blushed. "Except here it's you who has the accent." She chuckled. "Why can't you tell anyone you like opera?"

"My friends would think it uncool. Squaresville. And old. Surfers are all about rock and roll."

"I've heard the Beach Boys on the radio."

"I love the Beach Boys and Jan and Dean. Yet there's more to surf music. Have you heard of Dick Dale? He plays rapid-fire, reverb-heavy guitar. It's as if radical surfing, whether big waves or hot-dogging smaller ones, were a dance, and he's providing the music. But the Ocean has a serene side. A group called the Sandals makes music that captures the tranquility of the sea." Sonny smiled at her. "It's like a surfing slow dance after fast dances."

"We do know about the British guitar group, the Shadows. My father has a big record collection. He says saltwater sprays in your face when you listen to Wagner's *Flying Dutchman Overture.*

"Heda! Heda! Hedo!" Sonny shook his fist as he sang.

"I can't say I just met an opera singer," she laughed, "You're my first American surfer." She blushed and looked away, "You're the first American I've ever met, period." She snickered. "Are they all like you?"

"One of a kind," Sonny smiled and pointed at himself. "I came with an American friend. His name is Spence. He's nothing like me. He's a little older and more of the strong, silent- serious type." Sonny relaxed his shoulders and admired her eyes. "He keeps me in line."

"We do get South African surfers visiting from Cape Town and Durban. You're the first overseas surfer to visit my church. We usually get British and German tourists. Most are sport fishermen or here for a wildlife safari."

"I'm here on a surfin' safari," Sonny beamed. "Is this your church?"

"It's my father's. He's from Germany and a Lutheran. My mother is an Afrikaner from Pretoria. He learned the language from her. We have services in English, Afrikaans, and German. We also witness to Topnaar villages. Their native tongue is Khoisan."

"What languages don't you speak?" Sonny sat down in the front pew.

The woman blushed. "I'd better start with basic English and apologize for not properly introducing myself. My name is Alicia." She extended her hand. "Alicia Muller."

Sonny held her hand and started to bend to kiss it. "Umm…" He released her hand. "I'm Sonny Dyer from California. I'm the unofficial World Champion Surfer." He folded his hands behind his head. "I say unofficial because I won the Malibu International. It's the World's most important Surfing competition."

"Lekker! I'm honored to meet you." Alicia beamed. "We have tremendous surf on our Skeleton Coast. I don't dare swim in the ocean. It's too cold, has dangerous currents, and Blue Pointer sharks." Alicia held the candle lighter in front of her. "Moreover, there's no one to help you should you get in trouble." The candles cast shadows on both of their faces. "I know from the Bernadette Hennesey and Johnny Bright movies that California has excellent surf. South Africa has surfing competitions. We don't. You must have another reason for coming."

'She's looking at me. Her eyes, those baby blue eyes. So different from Sammi's brown eyes. And her hair…Penny had blonde hair, but her hair is a whiter shade of pale.' Sonny took three deep breaths. 'Come on, Sonny. Get over Sammi.' He gazed into Alicia's eyes. "Okay, you promise you won't think I'm crazy…" 'She's beautiful in a different way than Sammi,' Sonny scratched his head. 'And Alicia has a mysteriousness.' "One night while walking on the beach with my buddy Spence, I didn't tell you he's a famous professional wrestler known as the Golden Surfer, we met this…Okay…We met a mysterious man who told us of a place on your Skeleton Coast called the Golden Strand. Have you heard anything about such a place?"

"No," Alicia sat down next to Sonny. "My country has gold deposits, although not mined as much as in South Africa."

"Alicia, I wish you were there to hear him describe it. He told us that somewhere on your Skeleton Coast, when the berg wind blows just right, it erodes billions of gold particles from the escarpment and sprinkles them into the ocean. The weight of the gold causes the surf to break into perfect tubular curls. It colors the sea gold and gives the spray a kaleidoscope of colors. Here's the best part. If you surf the wave and get barreled in, meaning the tube covers you completely, you emerge in a Heavenly semi-aquatic wonderland called Sonoria." Sonny closed his eyes. "Try not to laugh."

"Why would I laugh? I must learn other languages, and I just learned a new word in surfer, *barreled in*," she chuckled, "Learning about other cultures is part of my calling- reaching people for my Lord and Savior Jesus Christ. Are you a believer?"

"I was truthful about why I am here in Henties Bay. I'll also tell you the truth about my beliefs. I was raised a Christian, but I'm afraid I've drifted away. So much has happened to me lately, not all of it good." Sonny gritted his teeth. "At this point, I'm open."

Alicia looked into his eyes. "My intuition tells me you'll find what you're looking for, even if you don't know what it is yet. The Golden Strand is plausible as a natural phenomenon, as for Sonoria, well, far from being crazy, you're in good company. Great European explorers such as Juan Ponce De Leon, Ignatius Donnelly, Francisco Orellana, and Sir Walter Raleigh have searched for El Dorado, Shangri La, Atlantis, and the Fountain of Youth. Will you find this Sonoria?" Alicia shrugged, "Who am I to say you won't?"

"Isn't what you search for, Christian Heaven, the same thing?"

"No, Sonny," Alicia touched his hand. "I've already found it. You don't have to search; it's right here for the taking. Jesus paid a tremendous price for you to have eternal life in Heaven. The Bible gives us hints of what awaits. It's glorious beyond human imagination and understanding."

"But I must die first. I guess that's why the great explorers were so rabid about finding a paradise on Earth. I hope you can find time to tell me more.""I'm sure you know about the fall of man in the Garden of Eden.""Yes. My parents made me go to Sunday school.""The Garden of Eden is lost forever. Through Jesus, God and man are reconciled. We will find paradise in the afterlife." Alicia twinkled her eyes. "I hope I didn't just make you go to Sunday school. But I love sharing my faith."

Sonny stood up straight, shoulders back. "How about you tell me more over dinner tonight?"

"There's only one restaurant in town. They serve up some tasty local dishes, but you'd better learn about us by enjoying my mother's cooking." Alicia smiled. "How about I invite you to have dinner with my family tonight?"

Sonny beamed.

***

"Thank you very much, Hans, and let me again compliment your wife." Sonny stood with Alicia and her father at their front door. "I've never eaten or even heard of Bobotie. I don't know if it's always this delicious or if it's how she cooks it."

"It's our pleasure to share our cuisine with you." Hans stood as tall as Sonny but more stout, contrasting with his daughter.

"He's a champion surfer." Alicia stood next to her father while maintaining eye contact with Sonny. "I don't have to tell you how perilous our ocean is, but just exploring our coast is dangerous. I'm sure others advised you to take extra water, food, fuel, and a first aid kit. You will be out in the middle of nowhere. Also, be aware that the indigenous people have long memories of the German conquest, and now South Africa has imposed Apartheid. Racism cuts both ways. You had nothing to do with conquest or Apartheid; nevertheless, you may encounter Topnaar tribes that resent you just because you're White. I'm worried about you, Sonny." Alicia raised her eyebrows while widening her eyes. "Please, take a guide with you. We know just the right man.

He speaks fluent English and Khoisan. He's worked with British and German tourists. He knows the land and has an uncanny sense of direction."

"He also has a knack for spotting wildlife," Hans added. "People settled in Henties Bay because the Ugab River is a water source. It also attracts wildlife. There's a crash of Rhinos living there."

Sonny gasped.

"Don't worry," Alicia chuckled. "Your guide will see them first. He'll meet you at your hotel tomorrow morning. Good luck and may God be with you. If you find the Golden Strand and describe it to others like you did for me, I'm sure we will get many more visitors." Alicia extended her hand.

Sonny delicately touched her hand, closed his eyes, and nodded.

***

Sonny walked into his hotel room.Spence was seated on the bed. "Sonny, where the hell were you?" He stood and handed Sonny a plate of food. "I ate dinner at Koos van der Merve's Eetplek. It's the only restaurant in town. I had him make a takeaway plate for you." He handed Sonny the plate. "Those sausages are called Boerewors. He cooks them over flaming coals. They're delicious."

"Thanks, but I already ate." Sonny gave the plate back to Spence. "You won't believe what happened."

"Tell me?" Spence put the plate of boerewors on top of their chest of drawers. "I hope it's good because I saved this especially for you."

"Hey, thanks anyway, but I met the most amazing young woman. She's almost indescribable. Ethereal even."

"You are making quite a transition. From a different gal every night, to becoming besotted with one you couldn't have, now is it for another 12,000 miles from home? Will she break your heart and send you another 12,000 miles? Maybe the Japanese Coast this time? I heard they've discovered surfing."

"No." Sonny shook his head. "Her name is Alicia. She has the same poise and grace as Sammi, but she's personable and approachable. Alicia seems to float like an angel. You've got to meet her. She has long blonde hair, even whiter than Penny's, and wavy. She's smaller than Penny or Sammi. Alicia is more like a precious doll. She reminds me a little of the Golden Age of Hollywood movie star, Veronica Lake."

"Veronica Lake? Come on, Sonny." Spence grabbed his arm. "Let's not trade one obsession for another. We're here for a reason." Spence gripped Sonny's shoulders and looked into his eyes. "Princess Dorabella will make you forget Sammi and this new girl. So, get a good night's sleep. Tomorrow, first thing, we look for the Golden Strand."

"I have good news for you. Alicia's father set us up with a guide. He says he speaks the native language and is an expert on the terrain."

"Each time I think you've gone off the rails on me, you come through big time." Spence squeezed Sonny's shoulders and beamed. "A guide is exactly what we need. We're going to do this, Sonny. We'll find the Golden Strand and one of us will surf to Sonoria and the arms of Princess Dorabella."

Chapter 5

Spence and Sonny left through the De Duine Hotel's front door. They both stopped in their tracks. Their jaws fell open; their eyes opened as round as their mouths. Their hearts palpitated. Spence and Sonny skipped a breath. Bewildered, they looked at each other with rapid blinking. Spence spoke first, "Nangolo?"

"You answered your call." Nangolo nodded.

"How did you…?" Sonny turned pale.

"We have our ways. What's important is you." Nangolo pointed at them. "You are needed."

"This is impossible," Spence shook his hands.

"How impossible is your dropping everything to cross continents and oceans to be in my land?"

"A lot more possible than you appearing to us from the other side of the world." Spence shook his head. "At this point, there's nothing I won't believe. So, it must be you. First, let's get you something to eat." Spence smiled. "Come inside. The hotel serves a delicious breakfast."

Sonny clutched Spence's arm and moved his lips without speaking. "He can't."

"What do you mean, he can't?" Spence winced. "Oh, I understand." Spence turned to Nangolo, "When I am the king of Sonoria, there will be no injustice like here." Spence chuckled, "No matter what Dorabella says."

"Nangolo, you somehow, and I'll never know how, transported yourself 12,000 miles to convince us to travel

12,000 miles." Sonny stepped forward. "Why don't one of your people go to Sonoria and marry Dorabella?"

"We are a people of the land. You are men of the sea. Many foreign men on ships have crashed and died in our waters. You two do more than sail on the sea, you make yourselves part of the sea." Nangolo smiled, "Our sea is your sea."

"Well, Woodie Guthrie wrote and sang, *This land is your land, and this land is my land.* That's New York to California," Sonny tapped Nangolo's shoulder, "not Africa. Alicia is right. This is your land. We need your guidance. Our Land Rover is parked right over there. Golden Strand, here we come."

***

Spence drove on the beach southward for seven miles.

"Stop here!" Sonny pointed toward the ocean. "Wow! Will you look at the size of those waves? They're as big as Waimea Bay or Mavericks."

"I don't know, Sonny, they look angry. What do you think, Nangolo?'

"Now you understand why the Topnaar are a people of the land."

Spence walked to the shoreline and stared at the surf. Sonny stayed behind, waxing his surfboard.

"Not only are those waves big and angry, but Waimea and Mavericks have a shore patrol." Spence's surfboard remained in the Land Rover. He put his hands on his hips. "If anything happens out there, we're history. What do you think, Nangolo? We can't do Sonoria and Dorabella any good if we die."

"You didn't come 12,000 miles to go candy ass on me, did you Spence?" Sonny held his surfboard under his arm. "Safety first is for grammar school kids and sissies."

"Who's the candy ass when I'm bailing you out of fights because of your big mouth? Well, I got to take a piss, maybe that will help me clear my head." Spence walked toward the dunes. He found a Dollar Bush and relieved himself on it. A black snake perched in its twigs stared at him. "What are you looking at? You've never seen a human taking a piss?" He tilted his head at the snake. "You don't look so mean. Besides, you don't have a diamond-shaped head." The snake opened its jaws and hissed. "Oh, you have a black mouth. I once lived in Florida. I saw lots of Cotton Mouths. Your mouth is cotton's photographic negative. I know from cotton mouths that it's all show, so I know you won't bite." The snake flattened and raised his body, bared his fangs, and hissed. "Oh, now I know the problem. You didn't want me to piss on your bush." Spence zipped up his wetsuit. "Well, I'm finished." The snake hissed again; fangs extended. Spence walked away.

"Hey, Nangola, one of your creatures, a black snake, gave me a hard time. It seems he didn't like me pissing on his bush. I don't think he's venomous. The general rule in America is that a venomous snake has a diamond-shaped head. His head was coffin-shaped. The inside of its mouth was ink-black. America has a venomous snake that flashes cotton white as a warning. He hissed at me and bared his fangs, so maybe he is venomous."

Nangola bolted into the Land Rover, closed its windows, and locked the door.

"Hmm, well, Sonny, it looks like Nangolo knows something we don't. I think it's a sign to give this spot a miss and look for the Golden Strand elsewhere tomorrow."

***

"We didn't get a lot of searching done today." Spence carried his surfboard under his arm while walking up the steps of the De Duine Hotel. "As soon as I put this away, shower up, and change, I'm going to Koos Van Der Merve's for dinner. Join me. He serves his traditional dishes. The food's tasty."

"Could you take this for me?" Sonny handed Spence his surfboard. "I really need to see Alicia."

"Her again?" Spence took Sonny's surfboard. "Did you venture 12,000 miles to clear your head of a woman only to get hooked on another?"

"It's nothing like that, Spence. I want to find out more about Nangolo."

"Suit yourself. I'm cleaning up and getting some dinner."

***

Still wearing his wetsuit, Sonny ran to the church. He pulled on the door. *'Locked. Dammit!'* He looked in each window. *'No one.'* He sprinted to Muller residence. Arriving at the Dutch-style home, he banged on the door, taking its hinges to the limit. The door resonated like a timpani drum.

Alicia's older brother Leon answered the door. He stood over Spence, flared his wide shoulders, and looked down at him. "What's the big idea of banging on our door like the Gestapo or KGB? Did my sister invite you?"

"No." Sonny felt himself shrink. "Please, Leon. I need to talk with her."

"What do you want to talk to her about?" He put his hands on his hips.

"It's okay, Leon." Alicia pushed past him.

Leon scowled at Sonny before going back inside.

"I'm twenty-three years old, but he'll always think of me as his little sister. Besides, you shouldn't have banged on our door like you're the police or the army. Sometimes the government doesn't like what we preach. It's nowhere near as bad here as the Soviet Union; nevertheless, we get nervous when government officials visit."

"I'm sorry. I must talk to you about something." Sonny opened his eyes wide. "It's Nangolo."

Alicia took a deep breath and lowered her head. "You better come inside." Alicia led Sonny to a table in their living room. After they sat, a black servant brought them tea in ceramic cups with saucers.

Sonny took three deep breaths. "You know why I am in your country. I told you about a mysterious man Spence and I encountered back in California." Sonny closed his eyes. "The one who told us of the Golden Strand?" Sonny perused Alicia's expression. "Please don't mock me. That man was Nangola. I know you think I'm crazy. Believe me. It was him." Sonny shook hands.

"You're not crazy." Alicia squeezed his hand. "You're in Africa. A visitor can never fully understand the mysteries of Africa and its people." She narrowed her eyes. "I've lived here all my life; my ancestors settled here before Columbus landed in the Americas. I don't know if Nangola appeared to you physically or if he tapped into your spiritual energy and appeared to you intrinsically."

"You're right. I don't understand."

"The spiritual world is forbidden to mortals. The scriptures tell us our opposition is powers and principalities. We must trust the Holy Spirit to lead and deliver us from evil."

"If Nangolo is evil, why did you hire him as our guide?"

"Nangolo is not evil. He is his tribe's shaman. His people revere him. He serves a critical role in his tribe's culture and well-being. He has earned our respect."

"Didn't you say you preach to him and his tribe?"

Yes, I share the good news." Alicia folded her hands. "Nangolo is receptive to our message and allows me to share it with his people. Yahweh is a God of free will. I can only tell Nangolo and the Topnaar people the good news of God sacrificing his son as atonement for our wrongs and the gift of Heaven. It's up to Nangolo and anyone else to trust and obey the Holy Spirit. Nangolo may have contacted an alternative world forbidden to mortals." Alicia pursed her lips. "Or this alternative world may have contacted him. Whomever they are, Nangolo knows their distress. But I'm warning you. It's dangerous. Nangolo is an experienced shaman. You're not."

"Today, Nangolo helped us explore a part of your coast. I could sense he feared the ocean. He spoke of many sailors crashing on his shores. He told us he chose Spence and me because we make ourselves part of the sea rather than sail on it."

"Join me tomorrow." Alicia squeezed Sonny's hand. "I am bringing food and supplies to a Topnaar village. I will also read stories to the children." She twinkled her eyes. "You will learn more about Africa and its ways. In the meantime, stay for dinner."

"I want to stay, but…"

"I know what you're thinking," Alicia gaily laughed. "Don't worry. I'll call off the attack dog. Moreover, his bark is worse than his bite."

***

Sonny jiggled the key into his hotel room lock. Spence opened the door. "Sonny!" Spence hugged him. "Come over here and see what I brought you. It's Koos Van Der Merve's specialty. It's called potjiekos. Koos mixes lamb, vegetables, and spices in a cast-iron pot. He lets it simmer over an open flame. No stirring, the ingredients all blend." Spence lifted a metal dome cover over a plate. "Viola. Potjeikos!"

"What's gotten into you?" Sonny smiled. "You're never this nice to me. I already ate at Alicia's." Sonny raised his nose and sniffed. "But it smells so good that I must at least taste it."

"It's all because we're in this together. Eat up. Tomorrow, we find the Golden Strand."

Sonny pursed his lips. "Um…Spence…I'm sorry," Sonny lowered his head. "Tomorrow, I promised Alicia I'd go with her to a Topnaar village."

"You know what, Sonny?" Spence furrowed his eyebrows. "In the past, we were competitive with each other. It was always out of brotherly love. If Dorabella chooses you over me, I'll be happy for you. Now I don't know. I thought after 12,000 miles you'd stop playing pushover for female charm. Tomorrow, I will find the Golden Strand without you. After all, I will be her king." Spence pointed, "You would be her doormat.

Chapter 6

Sonny rode in the bed of a Volkswagen Type 2 single-cab pickup truck. Alicia sat in the front seat. Her older brother Leon drove. Jarring bumps on the dirt road straddling the Kuiseb river and glances at Leon's scowling face made it an uncomfortable ride for Sonny. He never noticed a pod of three hippos and a bask of five crocodiles. After thirty minutes of what seemed to Sonny like thirty hours, they arrived at the Topnaar village. Huts of wood, reed, and thatch were informally spaced. Goats and chickens wandered freely among the huts. Other goats were confined to pens. Hans pulled the pickup truck to a metal Quonset hut with an arched roof. Dozens of children ran up to greet Alicia.

"This is their school," Leon voiced his first words to Sonny. "My father's denomination built it. Help me carry these boxes inside." Lean pointed to two boxes. "They're school supplies. The other box contains children's books. Alicia will take them."

***

Twenty-eight young boys and girls gathered around Alicia. Each had a new book. Alicia read them Biblical stories from her copy. Sonny leaned forward and relaxed while watching Alicia. He raised his eyebrows and smiled. *'Amazing how she connects with children.'*

"Now you understand why I protect my little sister." Leon nudged Sonny. "She's beyond special."

"Yes, Leon." Sonny's gaze remained on Alicia.

Alicia closed her book and stood. "Children, there's someone I want you to meet. He comes all the way from

America. I know most of you are afraid of the ocean. Soon I will take you to the beach to see him become part of the sea. He doesn't just go into the ocean; he rides the huge waves on a board." Alicia smiled at Sonny. "His name is Sonny and he's the best surfer in the World."

"Yay!" the children cheered and ran up to Sonny, jumping up and down in front of him.

"Okay, kids." Sonny laughed. "I'm happy to meet you too."

***

The ride back to the hotel seemed easier for Sonny, although wind, engine, and road noise made it impossible to converse. Nevertheless, Sonny sensed less hostility from Leon.

Leon parked the pickup truck in front of the church. Alicia's father, Hans, greeted them. Hans and Leon went inside the church. Sonny and Alicia stood alone outside the main entrance. "I'm amazed at what I saw today." Sonny gazed into Alicia's baby blue eyes. "It was my most rewarding experience in years." Sonny beamed. "No. My most rewarding experience ever."

"Ministering to children is my calling from God. It's crucial to keep my word to the children. I promised I would take them to see you surf."

"First, I want you to see me surf." Sonny held her shoulders. "How about tomorrow? Besides, I want you to meet my partner, Spence. I hope Nangolo will be with us too."

"I'd like that." Alicia smiled and nodded.

"All right!" Sonny beamed. "Meet us outside the hotel at eight am. I'll take you inside and buy you breakfast."

Alicia pursed her lips. "I'd like that, but I'd feel uncomfortable and a bit guilty leaving Nangolo outside."

"I'll order to-go."

"Sounds like a plan."

Sonny gazed deeper. 'Such remarkable eyes. The angles and contours of her face. So beautiful.'

Alicia embraced Sonny for three seconds. "I'll see you tomorrow morning." She winked. After walking away for eight steps, she turned and looked back at him. She smiled, "Bye." She waved.

Sonny remained in a trance

***

The next morning, Sonny and Spence stood outside the hotel waiting for Nangolo. "I hope you don't mind, someone else is joining us."

"Someone else?"

"Yes. Here they come." Sonny pointed to an approaching Volkswagen pickup truck. He loped over to greet them. Nangolo disembarked from the passenger door. Sonny ran to the driver's side and helped Alicia exit. He took her hand and walked her toward the hotel. "Spence, this is Alicia."

Spence grimaced before nodding to her.

"Hi, Spence," Alicia waved to him. "Sonny has said so much about you."

"Sonny is right." Spence cracked a smile. "You do look like Veronica Lake."

"Who is she?"

"She's an American movie star, or at least she used to be. She was Hollywood royalty during the war."

"If she's a movie star, she must be beautiful." Alicia blushed. "Thank you."

"I'm sure Sonny told you we're here with a mission beyond just surfing."

"Nangolo has stayed hush-hush," Alicia looked at Nangolo. But Sonny told me about the Golden Strand. I never heard of it. Yet it is possible."

"I think you know that going with us is a bad idea." Spence grimaced.

Alicia blanched.

"But it seems okay with Nangolo," Spence nodded. So, just this once, it's all right with me."

Alicia sighed and wiped her brow.

***

"This is as good a place as any." Sonny turned to Alicia, who sat in the Land Rover's back seat. "We have an escarpment backing us. If the wind picks up, who knows? Besides, the waves are firing."

"Are you sure you want to surf here? It looks scary."

"When it comes to the ocean." Sonny beamed and pointed at himself. "I'm the king. Fear is not in my vocabulary."

"What he means," Spence looked back, "is that we're experienced and take every precaution."

The waves were double overhead. Alicia stood at the shoreline and watched with amazement. Spence shot the curl of a big wave, riding it straight to its terminus. Sonny caught an even bigger one. He performed a re-entry, waved to Alicia, and did a second re-entry.

Spence returned to shore first. Sonny shouted to Alicia before performing a handstand while riding a wave's whitewater to shore.

"We get surfers from Durban and Cape Town, but I've never seen them in action." Alicia placed her hand on Sonny's surfboard. "I never imagined anything like what I just saw."

"I did win the World's most prestigious title." Sonny raised his chin.

"Now I know why. Come." Alicia grabbed his arm. "Nangola has cooked us goat stew and hot coffee."

Nangolo, Spence, Sonny, and Alicia sat around a campfire. "This is how it started and how we got in this mess in the first place," Spence crossed his legs. "Sitting around a campfire with him." He chuckled while pointing at Nangolo.

"Even though we have wetsuits, I'm freezing. That ocean is colder than Northern California or Oregon in mid-winter. Throw another log on that fire. This place sure gets cold once the sun goes down." Sonny folded his arms. "A magazine wanted to sponsor me to surf Lake Superior in January. Burrrr...I don't think so." Sonny ate a forkful of goat stew. "I never imagined a goat stew could taste so good. Spence, I told Alicia about Nangolo appearing to us in

California. Well, Nangolo, we're all here. Care to tell us how you did it?"

"No. No." Nangolo held up his hands. "Some of my traditions and ways are only for me to know."

"Spence, Sonny, it's best that you don't know. It's not for outsiders to meddle with." Alicia looked at each of them. "And that includes me."

Nangolo then packed a ceramic pipe with dark green leaves and white powder. He took a hit and passed it to Spence. He took a deep drag, held it in, and handed it to Alicia. "No." She shook her head, stood, and walked away.

Sonny followed her. Spence glanced at them, took another puff, and handed the pipe to Nangolo. He took his turn on the pipe and handed it back to Spence

Sonny caught up to her. "I'm sorry, Alicia."

"I'm the one who should apologize. I've known Nangolo for years. I know his ways are different, but we've developed mutual respect. That stuff he's smoking is more powerful than you think. It's more than just weed. Smoking it is dabbling in the occult. I can't do it. Besides, it's illegal."

"Don't worry." Sonny laughed, "Who out here will ever know?"

"I know you are spiritually searching. God knows the number of hairs on our heads. He will know. Besides, it can take you to a dangerous place." Alicia tensed her lips and narrowed her eyes. "One you won't know how to get out of."

"I understand, Alicia. I don't need to smoke it either. My life was in a downward spiral before I came here. I want you to help me build it back up."

"The Chinese say that a journey of a thousand miles begins with the first step." Alicia chuckled. "You've journeyed twelve thousand miles. Choosing not to smoke that pipe and listening to me is your biggest step."

Sonny reached out and held her hand. She squeezed back. He turned to face her. "The natural beauty of the ocean and the stars is all the high that I need."

"The beauty of God's handiwork is awe-inspiring." She sat down and looked up. "I often look at the moon and the distant stars behind her. It helps me ponder the dimension that's Heaven."

Sonny sat next to her. "Is the moon a she?" He moved close enough that they touched. He breathed a sigh of relief because she didn't move away.

"Well, the Romans named her the Goddess Luna. I am a Christian, of course, but Latin language cultures such as the French, Spanish, Italian, and Portuguese refer to the moon as Luna." Alicia chuckled. "So, the moon," Alicia pointed to the sky, "is a she."

"Likewise, the next brightest celestial object," Sonny pointed skyward, "is the planet Venus. We can only experience the moon, planets, and stars from a great distance and only with our eyes. Yet we can experience the sea intimately and with all our senses. I love being part of the sea. Often, I wanted to conquer the sea. Now I know it's a challenge I can never win. The sea, like the sky, is eternal. All the oceans are connected and flow together. It's called the Thermohaline Circulation."

"You know so much," Alicia lay back. "I can appreciate how mortals can add to God's handiwork. As I look at the firmament, I can begin to fathom the artistry of Vincent Van Gogh's, 'The Starry Night.'"

"Yes. Van Gogh is my favorite artist." Sonny held Alicia's hand. "As a surfer, my favorite painting is Caspar David Friedrich's "Wanderer Above the Sea of Fog." I can now more identify with it after wandering 12,000 miles from home and experiencing your Cassimbo fog."

"But it's a lonely painting." Alicia rested the back of her head on Sonny's chest. "Now you're with me. Classical music, art, oceanography, I have a confession."

"What's that?" Sonny held her closer to him.

"When I first met you, I took you for a vacant surfer. You're nothing of the sort."

"Thank you," Sonny kissed her forehead. "No need for apologies. Aspects of the surfing culture are vacant and conformist. I keep many of my deeper interests secret as a result."

"Why care about what others think? Find one special person who appreciates the real you." Alicia smiled. "You can start with God. He gave you free will. Even the angels have free will. Evil men have taken free will from others. Why let people you regard as friends take it from you? I find the depth of your interests fascinating."

"Hey, you two," Spence walked over to them. "I'm going to sleep."

Alicia stood. "Sonny, would you mind sleeping in Spence's tent while I take yours?"

"Yeah, sure," Spence brushed off sand from his body, "but, unfortunately, he smoked that pipe with Nangolo. That means he's going to fall asleep first. I can never sleep over his snoring. You'd better get a head start on sleep because otherwise, his snoring will also keep you awake."

Sonny and Alicia walked to Spence's tent. "I heard what you said, Sonny. If it will make you feel better, I'll tuck you in, tell you a bedtime story, and sing you a lullaby so you can fall asleep first."

"See what I must put up with." Sonny looked at Alicia and shook his head.

Alicia laughed.

***

"Wakey, Wakey." Alicia opened the flap of Spence and Sonny's A-framed tent. "Surf's up."

Sonny climbed out of the tent. "Good morning, Alicia." He shook her hand and looked at the sea. "Hey! You're right. The surf is cranking." Sonny kicked over an upright pole, collapsing the tent.

"What the…" Spence crawled out of the tent.

"You can stop your snoring and join me for a session. I'm stoked. The surf's whaling."

***

Spence left the ocean first. "Nangolo, what kind of wind do you expect later this afternoon?"

Nangolo held up a smoldering log. "It's an Easterly. It won't get any stronger."

"That means we won't find the Golden Strand today. I know you must return. Alicia, as soon as your boyfriend finishes surfing, we'll pack up and leave."

Alicia blushed.

***

After returning to Henties Bay, Sonny walked with Alicia to her pickup truck. He faced her and put his hands on her shoulders. "I want to thank you for a special time."

"I had a great time too." Alicia smiled. "I learn something new each time I talk with you."

Sonny stared into her eyes for three ethereal seconds. He embraced her and kissed her lips. His tongue met a dental blockade.

Alicia lowered her head and blushed. She silently walked to her pickup truck. She waved to him as she drove away with Nangolo.

Spence watched from a distance. He put his hand on his hips and nodded. "Ahh-hah."

Chapter 7

Spence and Nangolo waited in the idling Land Rover. Sonny walked out of the De Duine Hotel and rubbed his eyes.

"It's about time, Sonny." Spence grasped the steering wheel and shifted the Land Rover into gear. "The wind is blowing straight offshore. Hurry up before it turns Easterly."

"I'm sorry, Spence. Today I'm taking a pass on surfing,"

"What do you mean you're not going with me?"

"I'm spending the day with Alicia."

"What?" Spence deployed the handbrake and sprang from the Land Rover. "We have a mission. We've traveled 12,000 miles to accomplish it." Spence moved six inches from Sonny and prodded. "We finally put Sammi Wray behind you. She was too uppity to even kiss you." Spence put his hands on his hips and jutted his head. "This time you're abandoning me for a prude."

Sonny slugged Spence in the jaw with a straight right. Spence staggered back three steps. He lurched forward, grabbed Sonny's right wrist, twisted it behind his back, and shoved him face-first onto the pavement.

Sonny climbed onto his hands and knees. He glanced at the blood dripping from his nose. He stumbled to his feet and faced Spence. "So, that's how you want it?" He wiped blood away with his right hand. "Nangolo said Dorabella would choose only one of us, and only one could enter Sonoria. You go." He pointed. "How many great explorers have searched for Heaven on Earth? Did any of them ever come close to finding it? How many philosophers and political leaders thought they could create utopia on Earth? Move to the Soviet Union and experience the result. The Garden of Eden is lost forever. Find Jesus," Sonny gasped. "And find Paradise after you die."

"I understood your infatuation with Sammi. She was beautiful, classy, and intelligent. I get it. You weren't used to rejection. I got that too. Yet I thought you learned." Spence threw up his hands. "I guess not. You let a cute little townie brainwash you with her religious nonsense." Spence put his hands on his hips and hunched his shoulders. "Go tell her I'm not waiting until death."

"I have the free will to believe what I want. Seeing how little you appreciated Penny, even if Dorabella exists and you find her, what makes you think you won't tire of her too? Suppose her beauty does exceed Penny, Bernadette Hennesy, Alicia, and Sammi Wray combined? Is that all you want? God gave the angels free will. A third of them rebelled. In what realm is this Dorabella perfect? Sonoria? Go find it without me."

"When did you become Mr. Preacherman?" Spence prodded. "And don't bring Penny into this. She's gone, and she may never be the same." He scowled at Sonny. "And it never happens if you didn't talk me into bringing her to the set."

"What Feldman did to her was diabolical. Thank God you were there to end it. But if you truly cared for Penny," Sonny prodded, "you would've gone 3,000 miles to West Virginia to help her instead of 12,000 miles looking for better."

Spence glanced at Nangolo. His blank expression looked more contemplative than apathetic. Spence sharpened his focus on Sonny.

"Maybe Dorabella and Sonoria do exist. Alicia made me realize spiritual realms do exist. It's also dangerous for mortals. Even if the skeptics were correct and we owe our existence to the Big Bang and evolution, the Golden Strand as a natural phenomenon is plausible and would prove a magnificent sight and experience." Sonny turned and walked away. "Go find it."

"Come back, Sonny. Don't leave me. I need you." Spence's eyes moistened as Sonny walked away. He shouted, "I love you, brother."

Sonny raised and lowered his arms without looking back.

Spence returned to the Land Rover. Nangolo looked straight ahead. "Nangolo, take the day off. I want to be alone. Besides, yesterday's spot was as good as any. I remember how to get there."

Chapter 8

Spence sped the Land Rover southbound along the beach as if jockeying a racehorse, except he was wearing the blinders. Frayed emotions numbed jolts from humps and jars from holes. Memories of the previous weeks flashed in his mind but failed to hold. He looked to his left and saw a familiar escarpment. The offshore wind blew stronger than on his prior visit. The surf rose to a twelve-foot face. Its smooth curls broke in sets of three. He stopped the Land Rover, disembarked, and hastily donned his wetsuit. His bladder ached. '*Better not piss in the ocean. The way my luck is going, it will attract Mr. Gray Suit.*' He walked over to a familiar dollar bush and relieved himself. He heard an angry hiss. "Not you again."

The black snake arched up, flattened its body, and displayed a coal-black mouth.

"Shut your mouth. If you were a cottonmouth, you'd be the family black sheep. What's the matter? Can't share your bush?"

The snake struck photon quick. Its head got stuck on Spence's wetsuit sleeve.

"You dumb son-of-a-bitch." Spence knocked the snake away. It fled through the brush. '*You're one fast bastard. Keep slithering. You slimy punk.*' "Hey, Mister Snake," Spence shouted. "You're forgetting something." Spence pulled a broken fang from his wetsuit sleeve, held it up, and shook it. '*I don't know if you're dangerous, Mr. Snake, but thanks to you, Mr. Wetsuit,*' he tapped his sleeve, '*we'll never know.*'

Spence returned to the Land Rover and grabbed his surfboard. A wave of nausea hit him. He keeled over and retched. "Damn, Spence," he spat out metallic-tasting puke and saliva, "don't let Sonny upset you." Feeling lightheaded, he spun his head around twice. "Woo." '*I thought I slept off Nangolo's pipe.*' He turned and faced the escarpment. "Wind, wind, beautiful wind. Come on, blow harder." He felt shortness of breath. "Thanks for listening, wind." He opened his mouth so the wind could blow air into his lungs. As the wind intensified, Spence saw a wall of dust bearing down like an express steam locomotive. Shock and awe froze him. Three seconds later, particles stung his face. He squinted at the cloud's golden albedo. Rays of red, orange, yellow, green, blue, indigo, and violet now danced in the golden light. He turned toward the sea. The golden cloud had blocked out the sun, yet the ocean glowed. *'This is unlike any dawn or dusk I've ever seen. It's not orange, yellow, or red. It's pure gold!'* The waves had become tubular curls, breaking slowly from north to south. Spence looked to his left. He saw vortexes of color inside the curls. He grabbed his surfboard and shouted, "Yahoo! The Golden Strand! I found you!" He sprinted to the shoreline. *'No human has ever seen such waves. Now I'm gonna surf 'em.'* He felt like a jet taking off from an aircraft carrier as he leapt into the ocean with his surfboard. An outgoing current swept him to the break. Euphoric, he sat on his surfboard. A set of golden surf rolled in. The first wave rose. He stood and slid into the pocket. The curl barreled over him. He heard a chorus of ethereal female voices above the ocean's roar. Prismatic colors swirled before him in a funnel. He surfed into the opening…He no longer skimmed over the water's surface but flew. A cloud of golden fog shrouded him. The female voices sang louder… She stood in front of him with open arms.

"Oh my God, Her skin! It's glowing like molten bronze. Her hair, oh, such gorgeous long hair, like threads of gold."

Her gossamer, delicate, and silky attire featured a swath forming a thin "V" that started at each shoulder, matching the shape of her figure. It ran across her breasts to a gold waistband with a horizontal strip covering her nether region. Her cheekbones gave her face a delicate look, contrasting with her athletic body.

'Those copper-colored eyes…They're misty and wide open. She's smiling at me. Her cheeks, so soft; her lips, so inviting, so exciting.'

She raised her long, toned arms. A force stronger than gravity drew him to her. They embraced and kissed. Her lips felt smoother than rosebuds. Each flick of their tongues played a violin sonata. She pulled her head back and smiled. "You have arrived. I waited so long, Spence. I am Dorabella." She took his hand and stood beside him. "Swim with me to our palace in Sonoria. You can now breathe both underwater and air. Come. I want to make love to my new king."

***

Sonny stopped at Koos Van Der Merve's Eetplek. Koos's radio played Jim Reeves' *Welcome To My World.* "Ak Nee Man," Koos walked around the counter. The top of his round, balding head reached Sonny's bleeding nose. "What happened, mate? Did you fight Henry Cooper or Cassius Clay?"

"It's nothing," Sonny winced, "just a little scuffle."

"Did you win?"

"Does it look like it?" Sonny sniggered. "Can I use the restroom to clean up?"

Koos nodded and pointed at the restroom door.

After cleaning up with soap and water, Sonny left the restroom.

Koos pointed to a plate with two sausages and toast. "Boerewors, on the house, we gotta beef you up so you can win your next fight."

"Boerewors? My friend Spence told me all about them." Sonny winced. "Or should I say, former friend?" He dropped his head. "He's the one I scuffled with."

"You fought Spence?" Koos chuckled. "I don't know if you're brave or stupid. Well," Koos left for the kitchen. He returned with a boerewors impaled on a grill fork. "You better eat more if you're going to fight blokes his size." Koos put the sausage on Sonny's plate.

***

Each step closer to the Good Shepherd Church raised Sonny's spirit. His walk became a lope as he entered the church grounds. He grasped the front door. *'Unlocked.'* She sat in the front pew. He beamed. Sonny slipped down the aisle. He stood still until she finished her prayer. "Alicia."

She looked up at him. "I thought you'd be looking for Dorabella with your friend?"

"That's a long story." Sonny grinned.

Alicia stood and faced him, "About last night." She blushed and lowered her head.

"What about last night?" Sonny smiled and raised his hands.

"You know…" Alicia took a deep breath. "Things happened that shouldn't have."

"What are you talking about?" Sonny placed his hand on her shoulder. "Nothing happened."

"Nothing happened!" Alicia knocked his arm away. "So, because I didn't sleep with you like the tarts you're used to picking up, it was nothing?"

"It's not that." Sonny raised his palms.

"Then what was it?" Alicia prodded. "Who do you think I am? A docile little church mouse or an angel untouched by a man? Sorry to disillusion you. There's much you don't know. You probably think Nangolo is some ooga-booga witch doctor. Breaking news. There's a lot more to him. Do you know what was in the pipe he smoked with your mate?"

"Yeah, it was just weed. What's the big deal?"

"Just weed, huh?" She nodded and winced. "It was what's called a 'white pipe.' The 'just weed' is known as Durban poison. It's high-potency cannabis cultivated in the Drakensberg Mountains outside of Durban. Illegally, may I add?" Alicia put her hands on her hips. She hunched her shoulders, "and later smuggled into my country. Did you notice the white powder? That was ground-up Mandrax tablets. Mandrax, in case you didn't know, is a powerful narcotic. It's illegal unless doctor prescribed. Its active ingredient is methaqualone. Anything above a medically prescribed dose causes hallucinations. For many, powerful and uncontrollable hallucinations. Combined with Durban poison, it's as powerful as LSD. That's lysergic acid diethylamide in case you thought I didn't know. The effects of a white pipe can last long after you think it wore off."

"I didn't know." Sonny turned pale.

"It's my business to know. There's much you don't get. The Lord's house is no place to teach you." Alicia prodded. "So, get out!"

Sonny blanched. His jaw chattered.

"Now!"

Sonny turned and left. He walked with his shoulders slumped, head bowed.

***

Sonny stood at the shoreline. Frigid water rushed over his feet. The surf was heavy and rough, crashing in angry closeouts. He spotted a rip current going well beyond the breakers. A collage of faces rushed through his mind. He saw his parents. *'You're a disappointment, a surf bum who's not amounting to anything.'* He saw the faces of the girls he had used and left brokenhearted. He saw Sammi's image, the one who rejected and hurt him. He saw Spence, the only ever true friend he ever had, now lost. Lastly, he pictured Alicia. *'Do I love you, Alicia? I'll never know.'* Emptiness plunged into his gut. He waded until the sea reached his knees. The powerful current created 'V'-shaped eddies around his legs. The cold water had already numbed his feet. Sand rushed through his toes and over his ankles. He bent over, threw his arms back, and set to dive.

Chapter 9

Spence lay on a platform bed. Vines with technicolor flowers entwined the gold posts and gold canopy frame. Calm, shimmering golden waters lapped on the open bedroom's edge in a lub-dub cadence. A gentle sea breeze mingled with the fragrant aroma of flowers. Spence glanced at the horizon. He saw no sun, moon, or stars. Yet the sky glowed tourmaline, tanzanite, and sapphire.

Dorabella lay next to him on top of golden satin sheets. Desire overrode his senses. He kissed her mouth long and hungrily. She closed her eyes, enticing him to smother the contours of her face and the curves of her cheeks with wet kisses. He again kissed her lips. Three seconds later, he delicately nibbled her chin before kissing her round neck, its erotic aroma stirred his appetite for more of her lips, her tongue, and her sweet breath. He raised his head to admire her breasts. *'Perfectly round, so natural.'* He plunged his nose into her cleavage. Their scent ignited him. He cupped her right breast while kissing and sucking her left breast. He again kissed her lips, returned to her breasts, and moved to her abdomen. "Dorabella! Dorabella! I found you! At last, you're mine." He wound his arms around her lower torso.

"Spence, I waited so long. Let me feel you taste all of me."

He gripped her buttocks and lifted her hips so her mellow thighs could squeeze his cheeks. He munched on her golden filaments; his tongue slurped every droplet of her nectar. Her moans sounded like a choir, soon hitting a screaming crescendo. At last, she collapsed.

They gazed into each other's eyes and smiled. No words need be spoken. The grand moment had arrived. They united. Kissing her took on a new meaning. They cherished each stroke, each second. *'Forever my Dorabella... I will make this last forever, forever, and forevermore my queen.'* Forever arrived in pulses and pulses. Spence rolled over and gasped for air.

"Don't stop now. I want you again and again."

***

Dorabella stood beside their bed. She took Spence's hand and helped him to his feet. "Come." She led him to the bedroom's edge. "Look in each direction. Can you not see idyllic shores for as far as your eyes can see?"

"Yes, it's beyond just beautiful." Spence pinched his chin and thought, *'It all looks the same.'*

Dorabella scooped up a handful of golden water and poured it on his head. She walked to a jewel-encrusted teak bureau and pulled out a silky, golden robe. "Wear this for our feast. You may wear sandals, but the rocks will move before your feet strike them. Our people await us. Come with me to our wedding feast. By making love to me in our bed of gold, by allowing me to sprinkle golden water on your head, our God, the great Jari Kavumba, has united us for eternity. Now Sonoria will celebrate." She held his hand and led him across the gold-tiled floor through the palace's great hall. Its domed ceiling featured frescos of what looked to Spence as hybrids of Renaissance angels and mermaids. Gold-framed paintings of muscular sea Gods and lithe sea goddesses adorned the walls. Outside the palace, a clear pond with a finely crushed coral bottom and a fountain spraying dancing water centered the courtyard. Princess palms, queen palms, and tropical flowers deftly landscaped the grounds. Colorful birds chirped in harmony with the gentle breeze and fountain mist. They followed a path of gold granules. A soft wind fluttered her hair while wafting in the aroma of the sea, fruits, and flowers. They exited the palace grounds through a platinum archway. The pathway became finely crushed seashells. Mahogany and teak trees were interspersed with coconut and banana palms. Spence picked a purple frangipani flower. He sniffed it before putting it in Dorabella's hair. He looked into her copper eyes. He felt a twirling haze as he kissed her. "It's all so unreal, Dorabella. I can't comprehend all of this."

"Don't." Dorabella tapped his nose. "Just love me, rule Sonoria with me, and obey the great Jari Kavumba."

"Who is this Jari Kavumba?"

"Never question." She put her hands on his shoulders. "Just follow me and you will come to know." She kissed him before leading him by the hand.

***

A gray-haired man half Spence's height, dressed in white pants and a white shirt, greeted them. Dorabella and Spence stepped onto a podium. They stood behind a long balau hardwood table with intricate carvings and gemstones. Bowls of bananas, mango, papaya, pineapple, and other fruits and vegetables Spence had never seen or heard of sat on the table. A mass of people wearing white robes was before them. They stood behind long, unadorned, soft wood tables. The still sea behind the people was cobalt blue rather than gold, but had the same tanzanite and sapphire horizon. "Hail Queen Dorabella," The people bowed.

Their greeter stood before them and raised his hands, "Presenting our new King. Spence!"

"Hail, King Spence!" The people bowed. "Hail, King Spence."

Dorabella motioned for them to sit. "Let the feast begin. You may eat." She turned to Spence. "He is Delnoke. He is our chief advisor."

Two lithe young waitresses, one with a blonde ponytail and the other a brunette with long, straight hair, put domed platters in front of Spence and Dorabella. They lifted the dome, revealing steaming lobster, crab, and sea bass. Raw scallops, oysters, and clams sat on ice.

One of the waitresses put dipping sauces in front of Spence and Dorabella.

"I've never tasted anything like this." Spence held up a golden fork with a chunk of lobster.

"What do you think of our servers?"

"The young ladies?"

"Yes. Are they not comely and fair?"

"Yes, but they fall well short of my queen and my wife." Spence kissed Dorabella's lips.

"I know you are my king. I am not jealous. They are our servants; their duty is to serve and please us in every way."

"Both of us?"

"Whatever pleases you, my king." Dorabella smiled. "We are king and queen. Their names are Weena and Wanda. They are ours for our pleasure, another blessing from Jari Kavumba."

"But there's so much about Sonoria that's pleasurable. Like this fruit. I've never seen or tasted anything like this." Spence held up a blue tomato-looking fruit. "It's delicious just like the seafood, and," Spence chuckled, "you, my queen." He put his fork down. "Just one thing, I see the people only eat fruits and vegetables."

"Jari Kavumba only permits you and me to eat the sea's bounty. Our minions may only eat the fruit of the land. Only on special occasions that Kavumba chooses can they eat anything else."

"That's unfair. As king and queen, let's change that rule."

"No!" Dorabella blanched. "You must never question the mighty Jari Kavumba. Now comes the highlight of our feast." She beamed as the female servants poured a draft from a crystal carafe into Spence and Dorabella's goblets. "You will find this wine to your liking. Our minions will drink theirs with us. Only ours is made of the ambrosia from the forbidden domain of Kavumba."

Spence stood and raised his goblet to the crowd. They waited for Spence. They drank after Spence finished. He turned to Dorabella. "I'm a beer drinker, but this wine is amazing."

"It's from the vineyard of Kavumba himself."

"It gives me more than a buzz. I feel strengthened and invigorated.' Spence gazed into Dorabella's eyes. "Virile." He grinned.

"Our wedding feast is over." She extended her hand. "Shall we return to our marital bed?"

Spence beamed. She took his hand. They walked together.

Chapter 10

Spence slept deeply and soundly enough to render his world a blank and black void. He awoke to Dorabella kissing him. He felt disoriented. It took almost a minute for him to return her affection. "I didn't know where I was. Now I know I am in your arms."

"Your diaphragm stopped moving. I heard no breath. My kisses revived you." Dorabella stood naked beside the bed.

Spence marveled at her physical form. The morning light shone off her golden bronze skin. 'If only Sonny could see her. Penny? Sammi? Alicia? They're mortals. Dorabella is immortal. A Goddess. You passed her up, Sonny. Enjoy Nowhereville and your little townie.' Spence reached out, grabbed her hand, and pulled her back into their bed.

***

Spence and Dorabella strolled hand in hand from the palace grounds. Ten minutes later, they reached a clear lagoon of golden water with an inlet from a turquoise sea. A waterfall that Spence estimated to be fifty feet high cascaded into the lagoon at the other end. A hyacinth McCaw flew overhead. A toucan had perched on a hibiscus branch. The surrounding hills were flush with emerald-green trees. Colorful flowers interspersed the green leaves with flowering branches. Weena and Wanda took the robes from Spence and Dorabella. Both servant girls were already naked. *'Firm and fat-free. Smaller than Penny but bigger than Alicia. Beautiful but short of Dorabella.'*

"What are you waiting for?" Dorabella took Spence's hand and led him to the lagoon. She dove in.

Spence followed. The transparency of the lagoon made it a wonderland. Holding his breath, he swam toward the surface. Dorabella grabbed his ankles and held him back. She waved her finger in front of her face and shook her head. Spence inhaled a mouthful of water. He exhaled it. *'Oh my God! I can breathe underwater!'* Dorabella and Spence held hands while exploring the forest of staghorn, brain, and finger corals. Its variety of bright colors and spectacular fish enchanted him. They swam into deeper, cobalt-blue water. He became so relaxed and at one with the watery environment that he felt no threat from the six large sharks gliding around them. The sharks' pectoral fins were long and wing-like. Their pectoral fins, dorsal fins, and tail flukes were rounded with brilliant white tips. Dorabella and Spence made love among the sharks.

***

Spence and Dorabella lounged on the beach. Weena and Wanda served them lobster bisque and drinks in half coconut shells, complete with a paper umbrella jammed into a pineapple slice. Dorabella took the paper umbrella from the drink and teased Spence by tapping it on his nose.

Spence took the paper umbrella from her, rubbed it on her cheek, and sniffed it. "Do we always have this beach to ourselves? Where is everyone?"

"Kavumba has given this beach to us alone. It is forbidden to anyone other than us or our servants."

"Let's let the people enjoy this. Shouldn't the people of Sonoria enjoy its splendor?"

Dorabella smiled. "No, Spence, this is for us alone. Our minions could never appreciate this. Besides, Kavumba has willed it this way. We must never anger him by questioning his decrees.”

“But it’s not right.”

“Silence.” She put her finger over his lips.

“Look. There are some people.” Spence pointed to the volcano. “It looks like they’re carrying a dead body.”

“The volcano is Mount Kavumba. It is his domain. It is forbidden to all. After a minion dies, Kavumba permits the other minions to carry the remains up a designated path. They will cast their deceased into the volcano. Their vaporized body will rise with the smoke and be with Kavumba.”

“Where is Kavumba?”

“You ask too many questions, King Spence.” She pecked his lips. “You rule Sonoria with me. You need know nothing more.”

“But now I rule Sonoria. I want the minions eat seafood and enjoy this lagoon.”

“Silence,” Dorabella scowled at him. “You risk angering Kavumba. He can take everything away from us, and without a second’s notice.” Dorabella now smiled. “The good news is that our love will last for eternity. When one of us passes, we both enter the volcano together. Our smoke will mingle, and we’ll be united with Kavumba for eternity.

Spence gasped. “But that’s barbaric. In my World, marriage is until death do us part. I want you to be happy after I die.”

"What makes you think you will die first? Hush."
Dorabella placed her fingers over Spence's mouth. "Do you
want to live without me?"

"No…but…"

"Say no more."

"It appears Kavumba is quick to anger. Does he not love
us? I'm not religious." Spence spread his hands, "But I was
raised to believe that Jesus loved us."

"Don't ever say that name again." Dorabella turned to
see the volcano belch smoke. "Our love for each other is a
gift from Kavumba. He can take our lives at his whim. He
can force us to jump into the volcano together if we are
deemed unworthy of ruling his kingdom. He may boil us in
the lava for eternity. Now make love to me and thank
Kavumba.

Chapter 11

The instant Sonny dove into the frigid Benguela current, he knew he was trapped on a fast track to the open ocean. A dash of panic overrode his intent. He tried digging his feet into the sand and standing. An incoming wave knocked him back and held him underwater. He almost inhaled cold ocean water into his lungs as the salt stung his eyes. The turbulence shook him, further disorienting him. The wave pushed him toward shore. He was able to plant his feet into the sandy bottom and stand as the wave spat him out in shallower water. He crossed his arms over his chest and shivered. Inexplicably, a comforting warmth blanketed him. She stood on top of the ocean. Wings of shocking white feathers sprang from her back, in polarity to her tress of indigo hair. Her eyes were bluer than the deepest sea. A white gown cloaked a female body unsurpassed by even a masterpiece sculpture. Her cheeks and lips were florid like rubies and roses. The aroma of flowers drifted across the salty water. "Sonny. Return to shore. We have great plans for you."

"Who are you? You're more beautiful than any woman I've ever imagined. But your wings? You're not human. Are you Dorabella?"

"I am not Dorabella." The woman chuckled. "My name is Isolde Maria. One more step into the sea and you will be lost forever. Today, the abyss hungers for lost souls. Return to shore." The current ceased to flow. Sonny waded back to the shoreline.

"Who are you, Isolde Maria? You're so beautiful. Beautiful beyond imagination."

"I am from Heaven, where all is beauty, love, peace, and truth. Why do you do this? Your eyes were opening. If you had succeeded in suicide, you would have been lost forever."

"Yes, but life slammed my eyes shut yet again. What's the use?" He spread his palms.

"I am a Heavenly angel. I was created a level above humans. Have faith in the one who made us both, and you will be shown the way. Heaven has a purpose for you."

"What about Nangola? He used spiritual means to bring me here. Is he one of you?"

"Nangolo is human. He is searching just like you and Spence. He has yet to find. He used forbidden magic. Yet all things work together for the good. You do not yet have saving faith in the true God. We had to use Nangola to bring you here."

"If this happened a little over a month ago in California, I would check into a loony bin. After all that has happened, I'm ready to believe anything. I know you're real because creating you exceeds my imagination and artistic ability. So, please lead me to the true God and tell me my purpose?"

"That is not my commission. I shall therefore send you to a human who can lead you to saving faith. In God's time, you will learn his purpose for you."

"A human? Who?"

"Will you trust me, and do as I say?"

"I'm convinced you're an angel." Sonny chuckled. "If I can't trust an angel, who can I trust?"

Isolde Maria gaily laughed. "Return to Henties Bay and Koos Van Der Merve's Eetplek." The angel beamed. "The person whom I speak of waits for you there."

Isolde Maria vanished. Sonny breathed through his nose and imbibed the remnant of her floral aroma.

***

Sonny jogged into Henties Bay. He sprinted the rest of the way to Koos Van Der Merve's Eetplek. He yanked open the door. She sat at a table. Sonny stood still. She looked up at him and smiled.

"Alicia?"

Alicia stood, took Sonny's hand, and led him outside. She gazed into his eyes.

"I'm sorry, Alicia. I said things that I shouldn't."

"That's okay. It me some time, but now I understand." She nodded. "I also did something wrong."

"What was that?" Sonny shrugged.

Alicia kissed him on the lips; her tongue darted into his mouth. They embraced for a full minute. "Come inside." She motioned with her head. "It's potjiekos day. Koos makes the best potjiekoss in the world." Alicia chuckled. "Don't tell Leon or my father I said that."

"I wouldn't tell Leon anything he might not want to hear." Sonny laughed. "After lunch, can we go to your church? I have a long story to tell."

Alicia put her hands on his shoulders, gazed into his eyes, and kissed him. Koos Van Der Merve's radio played Jim Reeves' '*He'll Have To Go.*'

***

Sonny and Alicia sat together in a pew at her family's church. "Alicia, I confess, I was about to end it."

"End it?"

"My life, Alicia. I don't know if I came all this way looking for something or to escape. Everything about my life back home was spiraling out of control, down the drain. Just before the freezing ocean could sweep me away to oblivion…Please don't think I'm crazy, Alicia, but an angel appeared to me. A female angel. You must believe me. Do you?"

"Of course, Sonny. The Bible has many accounts of angels."

"Alicia, this angel was more beautiful than even the greatest artist could imagine."

"The Bible teaches us that angels are created a level above humans, so I believe she was as beautiful as you say."

"Thank you, Alicia." Sonny squeezed Alicia's hand. "Her name was Isolde Maria. I want to find the true God. Isolde Maria said I must go to the one who can show me the way. I believe she meant you."

"You do understand that all humans are fallen. We were given free will. Adam and Eve chose to disobey. As a result, all of us fall short of God's glory. God walked on Earth as a man. His name is Yeshua. We know him as Jesus. Only Jesus fulfilled his Father God's righteousness. Yet he was executed for our sins. He was resurrected from the dead and ascended to Heaven. Eternal life is his gift to us. Do you choose to believe on him?"

Sonny held up his hands. "My parents sent me to Sunday school. I was taught this. It seems simple, but I'm afraid I never understood."

"Even the greatest teachings are like a clanging gong if they lack love. Do you understand why God sacrificed his son and why the son willingly endured a horrible death?"

"It's a mystery to me, Alicia?"

"The mystery of love is greater than the mystery of death." Alicia tapped Sonny's hand. "Jesus solved the mystery of death by rising three days later. He died out of love for mankind, and he rose from the dead so one day we can live with him in Heaven forever."

"I was so wrong, Alicia. So wrong. I have done many people wrong. I have lived life only for myself. How can God love someone like me?"

"We are all wrong, Sonny. All of us. I know I need a savior just like you do."

Yes, Alicia. I want to take Jesus into my heart as my savior."

Alicia embraced Sonny.

Sonny gazed into Alicia's eyes. "Will we ever know the mystery of love?"

"Not every mystery is for us to know while we live on Earth. Our Heavenly Father will reveal them to us when we meet him in the next life." Alicia held both of Sonny's hands. "Yet until that final day, he will give us clues."

Sonny and Alicia's foreheads touched.

"I also want to pray for Spence. I don't know where he is. It must be dangerous for him to explore the Skeleton

Coast solo and to surf in your ocean alone, not that Spence ever shied away from danger."

"Where two are more are gathered in his name, he will be there. Of course, we can pray for Spence."

Sonny and Alicia held hands and prayed.

Chapter 12

Spence and Dorabella sat at a gold-gilded table carved from imperial jade. Their seats had purple, plush velvet padding. Set on a narrow tongue of land, the grass was full and trimmed like a golf green. The first fifty meters of water surrounding their peninsula had a glassy, clear jade hue. The next water line was aquamarine, fading to turquoise, and finally cobalt blue offshore. A tropical forest and the smoking Mount Kavumba volcano set the background. Dorabella wore a gown of gossamer-thin silk, dyed malachite green. Her five-meter capelet fluttered in the breeze. She wore her golden hair in a high beehive with long cascading locks. Spence wore matching swim shorts embroidered with wavy Sonoria tribal patterns. A female choir in lavender gowns sang them a vocalese. Weena placed two long-stemmed crystal goblets in front of them. Wanda poured from a sculptural decanter. Spence and Dorabella tapped glasses. Spence sipped. "I never imagined such beautiful voices. I was never much into classical music. Even so, I have never heard anything like those singers. Not on the radio, in a movie, or live. And this wine. It's delicious. What is it?"

"It is the nectar of the Bazenub fruit. It is only found on the highest slope of the great volcano. It is forbidden to all but us. Is not Bazenub nectar finer than any wine from your world?"

"Yes. Dorabella. It is delectable. Yet, you know I'm not much of a wine connoisseur. I'd give anything for a Lucky Lager."

"Much of your former world is profanity here. I have heard of this beverage you call beer. It is profane. Is not Kavumba's wine satisfying?"

"Yes, but…"

"Say no more." Dorabella held up her hand. Spence took her hand and nibbled on her fingers. She laughed. "Does your Lucky Lager beer have the same effect?"

Spence's brain tingled; his senses sharpened. He gazed into Dorabella's eyes. His mind registered that her skin tone and hair tint matched. He admired her long, feminine arms and the gap between her shoulders and chest. He hungrily kissed her. The taste of her mouth, lips, and tongue complemented the Bazenub nectar. A gentle sea breeze wafted in her perfume. He inhaled through his nose. "Why do I suddenly feel Helpless?" Spence rotated his head. "Oh my God! I love you, Dorabella." He dropped his head onto her upper thighs, muffling his voice, "I love you so much."

Dorabella nodded to Weena and Wanda. They refilled their goblets with Bazenub nectar. Dorabella placed her forefinger under his chin, raised his head, and looked into his eyes. "Sit up, Spence. Drink more. Drink to our love." Spence sat up, held his goblet, and tapped her goblet. Dorabella quaffed. She dropped her goblet. It shattered. "Say you love me. Say it over and over, again and again."

"Only if you never stop telling me you love me too."

"I was destined to love you before I was born. Kavumba had chosen you before your birth to rule Sonoria with me. I love you for all eternity. Never fear or doubt. We are united for both this life and the next life."

Spence saw the sea behind Dorabella glisten gold. He felt soft hands on each shoulder. His thoughts swirled.

Weena and Wanda were now naked. They started to caress his chest.

"Are you ready to enjoy them with me? Won't you please kiss them?"

"I love you, Dorabella. I love only you."

"I ask again, are they not comely and fair? Kavumba has selected them for us. Weena and Wanda are lovelier than any minion. They are for our pleasure. I love you, Spence. I would not deny you any of Sonoria's pleasures. Kiss them for me."

Weena first and Wanda second planted long, wet kisses on Spence's mouth. Spence kissed them back. He felt a hypnotic wave, "No Dorabella." He shook his head. "My desire is only for you."

"Do you deny me the joy our kingdom has to offer?"

"But are you?"

"Much of what is profane in your former realm is holy in ours." Dorabella winked. "That goes both ways, Spence. You are king. No one here will ever question your manhood. The rules of your former world don't apply here."

"No! I'm not…Please understand, Dorabella. My only desire is for you alone."

"I know your thoughts. You have many desires." Dorabella put her finger on Spence's lips. "Some you have kept hidden and buried deep in your subconscious mind. Now you know why Bezenub nectar is forbidden to the minions. Let your mind drift. I am your queen, and I will obey you. If you are not yet ready, you may take me and only me, and I will take only you." Dorabella kissed both Weena and Wanda with open mouths. "You two are dismissed. When the king and I are done, return to the palace."

Spence watched with glazed vision and felt a sparkle. He stood and took both of Dorabella's hands. Her flimsy gown fell to her ankles. She leaped and wrapped her legs around him. She gently bit his shoulder while he held her buttocks. He laid her on the grass and made love to her. Weena and Wanda sprinkled Bezenub nectar on them.

***

Spence and Dorabella walked along a pathway through a minion village. Each person they encountered dropped to their knees and bowed to them. "I wanted you to see their village. It is a gift to the minions from Kavumba."

Spence scanned the bamboo and grass-thatched houses. "They look comfortable enough in their simplicity. But how are they a gift from Kavumba? They seem easy enough to build."

"You must understand." Dorabella took both of Spence's hands and faced him. "His blessing goes well beyond the structures. Our idyllic climate turns simplicity into grandeur. We do not need rain as rivers from the mountains refresh our bodies and grow our fruit and vegetables. Do you see how they dip crystal decanters into the sea? Those decanters have magical powers to turn seawater into sweet water." Dorabella picked an orange and green-striped fruit resembling a mango from a tree. She took a bite from it and handed it to Spence.

Spence bit into the fruit. "Delicious. I've never tasted anything like it."

"We call it dagumboi. The minions may eat it as they please. We are about to gather in our grand assembly area for the Festival of the Hours. Tonight, we shall celebrate our blessings and bounties. We thank Kavumba for our perfect weather and clear water that keep everyone comfortable and safe. Tonight, the minions are permitted to partake of the bounty of the sea. In exchange, they will give him our annual gift of gratitude." She handed the dagumboi back to Spence. He finished it. Spence felt his chest tighten. He gasped for air.

"That happened to you last night," She grinned. "I can revive you." She kissed him deeply. Spence's chest began to swell and contract. Spence pulled his head back and smiled. He kissed her forehead and embraced her.

***

Spence and Dorabella stood behind the balau hardwood table. The minions were prostrate, chanting, "Hail, Queen Dorabella. Hail, King Spence. Hail, Queen Dorabella. Hail, King Spence."

"You may rise," Delnoke raised his arms. "Now be seated." He lowered his hands.

Dorabella stood and raised a scepter.

The minions chanted, "Jari Kavumba! Jari Kavumba! Jari Kavumba! Jari Kavumba!"

Dorabella lowered her scepter. "Let us honor our great God Kavumba with music."

Spence glanced at the orchestra. 'Those instruments? What are they? Some resemble violins but are shaped more like a bastardization of guitars and banjos played with a bow. The horns look like brass conch shells. The female singers are gorgeous like Weena and Wanda, but none match my queen.' Spence smiled at Dorabella.

Delnoke dragged what resembled a standing bass, but double the size. The instrument was pure white, matching Delnoke's attire. It had six strings rather than four. Delnoke raised his bow like a baton and waved it to the orchestra. They played a brassy, discordant number. Delnoke played his instrument in an atonal clash with the orchestra. Spence winced. *Delnoke's playing sounds like something from a sci-fi horror flick. I expect a flying saucer to land or the Kraken to rise from the sea.'* The instrumental music drowned out the soothing female choir. Before Spence could stick his fingers in his ears, the number ended. Dorabella's pupils opened wide. She beamed, "Did you enjoy our music?"

'It was a bunch of noise.' Spence smiled back at Dorabella. "I like the female choir most of all. Their voices are heavenly. I want to hear the vocalese they sang when I passed through the portal to your arms."

"Minion females are taught how to sing before they can talk. Voices play a crucial role in our culture. Males are taught to play musical instruments."

"I'm not much of a singer, and I can't play a musical instrument. But you inspire me to overcome my lack of talent and make music for you." Spence placed his hands on Dorabella's shoulders, gazed into her eyes, and sang, "Little surfer, little one, make my heart come all undone. Do you love me, do you surfer girl, surfer girl, my little surfer girl."

"You better stick to what you're good at," Dorabella chuckled, "like making love to your queen."

"I wish I could bring you music from my world. Elvis. Chuck Berry. The Beach Boys. Dick Dale. Rock and Roll. I miss it, Dorabella."

"I don't know anything about what you speak. I wish you could perform it for me. Based on how badly you sing," Dorabella chuckled, "I know you can't. Maybe Delnoke can play it for you."

"I don't think you understand." Spence sighed. "You can't teach someone to sing like Elvis or to play guitar like Chuck Berry."

"What's a guitar?" Dorabella placed her hand on his shoulder and blew minty breath on him. "The minions are good craftsmen. Describe it and they will make one." Dorabella put a gentle kiss on his lips. "Perhaps Delnoke can learn to play it like your Chuck Berry."

"You don't understand." Spence sighed. "It's in the blood, and it takes immense talent and practice. You can't just teach someone to play like Chuck Berry. Maybe Martin Denny or Jim Bacchi of the Tikiyaki Orchestra can teach your musicians something." Spence smirked. "Even that won't prove easy."

Dorabella grinned. "We can always make music together."

"What's happening now? The people are stirring. Delnoke is playing those eerie sounds on his weird-looking instrument. It sounds like I'm in the Twilight Zone or Outer Limits."

"The minions are preparing their sacrifice to Kavumba."

"A sacrifice to Kavumba?"

"Yes. A sacrifice to Kavumba. Look." Dorabella pointed to the volcano. "The Mount of Kavumba is billowing. We must appease him, or all you enjoy here will be lost. Our bodies and our love will be vaporized."

Spence's next sight and sound was eight men singing a somber chorus. They carried a thin, chesty woman with flowing red hair overhead. Her hands and feet were bound with colorful kerchiefs. Her mouth was likewise gagged. She squirmed and struggled against the bindings and tried to scream through the gag. "What is going on, Dorabella?" Spence looked back with dilated pupils, parted lips, and tense facial muscles. "What are they doing to her?"

"She is a virgin. They will carry her up the Mount Kavumba funeral path and toss her into the volcano. Don't fret for her. She will live with Kavumba for eternity, and Sonoria will be safe for another year."

"No! They can't do it. It's barbaric! Cruel!" Spence lunged toward them. "We must stop them."

"No, Spence." Dorabella grabbed his arm. "You must not interfere. Otherwise, Sonoria and our love will be lost forever."

"No, Dorabella. I am king. I won't allow it. I don't care if your Kavumba kills me."

"Stop!" Dorabella yelled to the eight men and held her arm in a halt gesture. "Put her down. Unbind her."

They complied.

"Come forward." Dorabella made eye contact with the girl and motioned to herself.

The girl took fidgety steps toward Dorabella and Spence.

"What is your name?" Dorabella steepled her fingers.

"Lola."

"Lola. Kavumba has granted you a choice. Do you wish to join him in the volcano, or serve your king and queen as our servant and pledge to please us as we ask?"

"I choose you, my queen."

Dorabella stepped forward. She embraced Lola and planted a long, wet kiss on her lips. Lola returned her affection.

Spence gasped.

"Wise choice. Delnoke will escort you to our palace."

"Why do you look at me that way, Spence? I have told you what may be profane in your world is holy in Sonoria. I waited many years for a king. I was forbidden under penalty of death and damnation to know a man. Kavumba permitted me to enjoy select female minion servants until your arrival. I will obey you, my king, and make love to only you. But do you deny me the pleasures of Sonoria?"

"No, Dorabella. It's not that."

"What is it?"

"You are making Lola a slave. Even worse, a sex slave. Knowing her in that way amounts to rape." Spence shook his hands. "Slavery is an atrocity. In my world, my country once fought a bloody war to end slavery."

"Lola chose to be with us."

"Lola had a choice between a fiery, painful death or living as a slave. How about we give her a third choice? Let her return to her people and one day be a wife and a mother."

"She will one day be a mother." Dorabella winked at Spence. "Only I am your wife. Lola joining Weena and Wanda is a great honor. Although we can do as we please with her, I know you will give her the gentleness and tenderness you've given me and I've given you. Do you doubt that she enjoyed kissing me?"

"How can anyone not enjoy kissing you?" Spence embraced Dorabella and kissed her. The people applauded.

Chapter 13

Spence and Dorabella walked hand in hand in fluffy sand along the shoreline. A pod of dolphins followed, often breaching and spinning in the air. "My love, my queen, my Dorabella, so much about Sonoria is enchanting. The wine here puts me in deeper trances, making comprehension even more daunting. And you, if any woman more beautiful than you ever existed, no camera has captured her image, no artist has painted her, no sculpture has modeled her. I have fallen deeper in love with you than God himself can permit a man to love. But how well do we know each other? What do you know about me?"

"I know the great Jari Kavumba chose you for me and brought you here to be my husband and king. Jari Kavumba permits you to love me with your entire being." Dorabella gazed into his eyes. "I love you with my entire being." She kissed him.

After five seconds, Spence pulled his head back. "But why is so much about you and this enchanted land secretive? I am used to it. My father was a defense contractor who dealt with the military's top echelon. He was forbidden to discuss his work with anyone, including his family. You don't even know what I did for a living in my world."

"Tell me." Dorabella arched her eyes.

"I was a professional wrestler. My profession keeps many secrets. We pretended to be someone we weren't. We faked fights for live and television audiences. Yet we had to guard our secrets or risk banishment from the profession."

"Is that why you came here? Were you banished for revealing secrets?"

"No. I kept our secrets. It's just that…"

"It's just that what?"

"Dorabella, I had women before you. The last one's name is Penny. Penny Williams. She was as lovely as a flower. Of course, she was only a flower." Spence chuckled. "You're the entire garden." Spence and Dorabella kissed.

"What happened? Did you stop loving this Penny Williams?"

"It's not like that, Dorabella." Spence kept his gaze on Dorabella's eyes and took a deep breath. "We had bit parts in a movie. One day, the producer, a vile yet powerful man, called her into his office. Dorabella." Spence closed his eyes and pursed his lips. "He violated her." Spence took a deep breath. "He didn't finish what he started, yet he inflicted horrific physical and psychological damage on her. She was traumatized. I don't know if she'll ever recover."

"Where is she now?"

"That's what concerns me. If you were to look up California girl in a dictionary, you would get Penny's picture."

"What's a dictionary?"

"It's not important." Spence bit his lip. "She's now living on a farm somewhere in the mountains of West Virginia. It's not just on the other side of the continent; it may as well be the other side of the galaxy. I can't fathom the extent of her trauma to make such a change."

"Why are you banished from your profession?"

"In rescuing Penny, I gave this individual what he deserved. I put him in intensive care."

"It sounds like you did the right thing as a man."

"Absolutely! And I'd do it again. Unfortunately, he is wealthy and powerful. He all but banned me from wrestling in California and made it almost impossible for me to work in any other entertainment field." Spence gripped Dorabella's shoulders and looked into her eyes.

"You say you're banned in California." Dorabella twinkled her eyes. "Can you wrestle elsewhere?"

"Dorabella, I have never told you my age. I am thirty-three years old. That's young for a man, but old for a professional athlete. I grew up in San Diego. California is my home. I love to surf, and I love the ocean. I can't see starting from scratch elsewhere. I was once the American Federation of Wrestling tag team champion with my buddy, Clayton Farnsworth. My promoter and booker had us lose the title in front of over 60,000 in the stadium and a national TV audience. My notoriety in the AFW was a bad guy. Clayton and I played onery outlaw cowboys. I returned home and played a good guy surfer. They dubbed me, 'The Golden Surfer'."

"You played yourself." Dorabell pecked Spence's lips. You weren't faking it." She kissed him with an open mouth. "You'll always be my good guy, golden surfer."

"Unfortunately, it didn't resonate with wrestling fans. In any case, my wrestling career was going downhill even before the incident."

"You may be washed up in California," Dorabella kissed him, "but you're king here."

"How about you, Dorabella? We now know how I became king. How did you become queen?"

"I became queen by marrying you."

"Before we married." Spence spread his palms.

"I was a princess from the day I came into being. I experienced little outside of palace grounds and ceremonies with the minions. I was my parents' only child. They taught me my duties as a princess and a future queen. One horrible day, my father was killed defending Sonoria from the Guerlocks."

"The Guerlocks?"

"The Guerlocks are a horrible, monstrous race that lives beyond the pink horizon." Dorabella pointed seaward. "They want to steal our bounty for themselves." Dorabella lowered her head. "After they murdered my father, my mother jumped into the volcano to join my father and be united with him and Jari Kavumba."

"Was she alive when she jumped in?"

"Silence." Dorabella put her finger over Spence's lips. "They are together. A man can be king of Sonoria without a queen, but a woman cannot be queen without a king. That is why you were summoned from your world to join me."

"The dolphins." Spence turned to the ocean. "They're gone." Spence turned ashen white. He pointed with a jittery finger. "Oh my God! It's a great white shark. So close to shore. I've heard fishermen and sailors tell tall tales about their size, but I never took their exaggerations seriously. This one is something out of a Japanese monster movie."

"What's a movie? You told me about this thing called a movie when you told me about Penny Williams. What are they?"

"Forget about it." Spence took four steps back from the water's edge. "That shark is scaring the daylights out of me. We're going to need a bigger beach."

"Relax. Her name is Carla." Dorabella chuckled. "She patrols our waters to protect us from the Guerlocks."

"But she's following us." Spence pointed. "She's looking right at us. I don't like it. What if she leaps from the water and gobbles us whole?"

"She has no taste for humans or Sonorians. She follows us to protect us. You are king. Carla serves you just like the minions serve you. She knows Jari Kavumba chose you. The Great Kavumba reached a human whom you call Nangolo. He knew where to find you and Sonny. But it was you who were chosen. Sonny was used to help bring you here to me."

"And if I try to swim away, will Carla have a say?"

"Carla's mission is to protect us from the Guerlocks. Otherwise, she will do as you say."

"Okay. I believe you. The oceanic whitetip sharks in the lagoon ignored us, and they're also a dangerous species." Spence sighed. "Dorabella, I love you so much, and so much about Sonoria is splendid. Yet I miss my family and my friends. I worry about Sonny. I acted as his big brother. I was his only true friend. We had a terrible fight before I found the Golden Strand and the portal to you. I would love to show you my world. When can we visit?"

"You ask too many questions. Don't you love me? Don't you appreciate all Sonoria has to offer?"

"Yes, but…"

"But nothing. I am yours, and you are mine. Let's go to the palace and make love. Lola, Weena, or Wanda can join us if you please."

"My desire is for only you, my Dorabella."

"And mine only to please you. I can't wait to get to the palace. Take me now.

Chapter 14

"Sonny!" Koos Van Der Merve lowered his spatula to his side. "You look a hundred times better than yesterday."

"And you know how to stir up a breakfast a thousand times better than anyone. I'll have the explorer's breakfast. Eggs, sausage, bacon, and potatoes, as only you can make them."

Sonny licked his lips to the sound of bacon and sausage sizzle.

Moments later, Koos placed a plate with Sonny's Explorer breakfast before him. "I hope you don't mind an extra egg, sausage, and two extra strips of bacon."

Sonny beamed and grabbed a knife in one hand and a fork in the other. Seconds before he could eat, he felt a soothing softness on his back. A pleasant floral scent mingled with his eggs, bacon, sausage, and potatoes. He turned. "Alicia!" Sonny stood. She wore sandals, tan slacks, and a white blouse. She twinkled her eyes. Sonny smiled. *'So, inviting her smile. So adorable. Her hair, her shocking white hair, in a ponytail.'*

Alicia kissed him. Sonny returned her kiss and hugged her.

"Kyk wat ek nou sien!" Koos dropped his jaw and circled his lips. "Alicia!"

Sonny wrapped his arm around Alicia's waist and faced Koos.

"You're one gelukkig bloke." Koos smiled at Sonny. "You be good to her. I've known her since she was a baby. She's a good one."

"The best." Sonny smiled.

"Alicia," Koos smiled, "no one ever called you fat. You better sit down and have yourself an explorer's breakfast."

"I should say, no thank you, I already ate. But I have been called maer."

"What?" Sonny asked.

"Skinny," Alicia chuckled. "So, Koos, if you can stir me up a breakfast that looks and smells anything like what you made for Sonny, I have to say, yes." Alicia sat at Sonny's table. After Koos put an Explorer's Breakfast in front of her, she bowed and said grace silently. She raised her head. "After we eat, get your wetsuit and surfboard. I have a special day planned for us."

"I'm afraid I can't. Spence took the Land Rover. He hasn't returned. I guess he's camping somewhere." Sonny pursed his lips. "I am worried about him."

"We have plenty of room for your surfboard." Alicia's eyes and head directed Sonny to look out the window. "There's our ride."

Sonny looked out the window and saw a small school bus. He had trouble swallowing when he spotted Leon behind the wheel.

***

Sonny and Alicia held hands as the school bus traversed dirt roads. With each bump, Sonny saw Leon's narrowed eyes and furrowed brow in the rearview mirror.

"I think you remember this place." Alicia pecked Sonny's cheek.

Leon stopped the school bus and opened the door. Alicia and Sonny disembarked. Topnaar children ran to the bus from all parts of the village. "He's back!" Alicia nodded toward Sonny.

The children mobbed Sonny and cheered. They jumped up and reached for his face. "I'm happy to see you all too." Sonny laughed.

"Everybody in." Alicia stood by the bus's door. "We have a special day ahead."

***

Alicia and Sonny rode in the front seat of the bus. Leon glanced back and glowered. *'Why couldn't she have us sit in the back?'* Sonny looked away.

"Here we are." Alicia stood and faced the children.

The children cheered and stormed out the door.

Sonny carried his surfboard under his left arm and held Alicia's hand with his right hand. Sonny stood in ankle-deep water and faced the children. "This suit protects me from the cold water. As you all know, the water here is too cold to swim without it."

"Get ready, kids," Alicia beamed. "You're about to see something you never imagined. First, let's all bow our heads in prayer." Alicia closed her eyes and bowed. "Heavenly Father, in the name of Jesus, please protect Sonny as he enters the sea. Amen."

"Alicia?"

Alicia blushed while smiling. "I almost forgot. Children. Let's all pray for Sonny's American friend, Spence."

"Yes, dear Lord Jesus." Sonny closed his eyes and bowed. "Please be with Spence and extend your loving hand

181

to him." Sonny looked up and smiled. "And I thank you for giving me the good surf to share my enjoyment of your creation with these children. Amen"

"Yeah!" The Topnaar children cheered.

Sonny rode a rip current past the break. He spotted an incoming swell. As it approached, he paddled furiously, racing it toward the shore. The swell steepened and started to break. Soony stood and slid down its face, soon riding in the pocket. Sonny performed a radical re-entry and then a 180-degree turn. The children on the beach cheered.

Rather than watching Sonny surf, Leon gathered driftwood. He stacked it in a pyre and cooked Boerewors.

Alicia waved to Sonny and gestured toward shore. Sonny rode the wash toward her. The children again cheered as he performed a handstand.

Alicia led the children in grace before they devoured their sausage lunch.

***

After returning the Topnaar children to their village, Leon drove Alicia and Sonny back to the De Duine Hotel. Alicia led Sonny by the hand. They stood behind the school bus. "Today was a blessed day for the children. It was also a blessed day for me." Alicia gazed into Sonny's eyes and blushed. "Thank you."

Sonny and Alicia kissed. They halted to gaze into each other's eyes. They embraced and kissed again. Sonny felt himself drift away. His euphoria faded like glowing specks of dust in the wind. Harsh jolts and electric bolts rattled his skull. The thud of his head against the school bus resounded like a kettledrum. Sonny could see the red veins in Leon's

182

eyes. Leon gripped him under his armpits and lifted him; he continued slamming him into the bus.

"Stop it!" Alicia pounded her brother with her fists. "Stop it!"

"I left Johan alone." Leon turned to Alicia, spraying spittle as he spoke. "And look what he did to you." He again slammed Sonny against the bus. "It's not happening again! Not if I can help it!"

"Stop It!" Alicia grabbed Leon's arm. "He's nothing like Johan. I'm twenty-three years old. I can make my own decisions."

Leon growled and slammed Sonny into the bus once more before dropping him and facing Alicia. He put his hands on his hips and jutted his head.

Alicia ran to Sonny and put her arm around him. She looked at her brother and prodded. "Go!" She furrowed her eyebrows. "Leave me alone. I'll walk home."

Lean grunted at them, turned, and drove away.

Alicia helped Sonny stand. She kept her arm around him. "Come. Let's go to Koos Van Dr Merve's." She licked her handkerchief before using it to wipe blood from Sonny's lip. "I'm sure you could use a cold Windhoek Lager."

Sonny took a deep breath. "I heard Windhoek Lager's slogan on the radio." He lowered his head and shook it. "It's not," he mimicked an American beer jingle, "Windhoek is the one beer to have when you're having more than one." His swollen lip hinted at smiling. "But I need more than one right now."

"I'll have one with you." Alicia winked. "Just one."

Chapter 15

Spence and Dorabella stood hand in hand at their palace bedroom's sea edge. "As long as I am alive, I will never tire of gazing at this horizon. My friend Sonny often talks to me about great artists. I wonder how Casper David Friedrich would interpret this Seaview. How would Vincent Van Gogh interpret Sonoria's nightscape? Could Leonardo da Vinci or Michelangelo paint a portrait of you?" Spence kissed Dorabella.

"Can you ever tire of making love to me?"

"Never." Spence chuckled. "But after our session on the beach," He gazed into her eyes and chuckled, "Well, I'm not Superman."

"Who's Superman?"

"He's a comic book Superhero who can do anything." He laughed. "Unless he's confronted with kryptonite."

"I don't know what a comic book is but follow me." Dorabella led him to a cabinet. She opened the cabinet and grabbed an elegant carafe along with two long-stemmed goblets. She handed him a glass and poured. They tapped glasses, linked arms, and quaffed.

Spence dropped the glass on the floor. It shattered. "I'm sorry, it's just that I'm feeling woozy, Dorabella, so woozy." Spence sat on the bed.

"Wait a moment." She laughed.

"Oh my God, yes." He stood. "I suddenly feel empowered."

"Do you feel like that Superman of whom you spoke?"

"Yes. I feel like Superman."

"I can see." Dorabella beamed. "Wait no longer. Take me."

Spence vigorously made love to Dorabella. "I love you, Dorabella, I love you." His mind switched from admiring her breasts and sculpted face with his eyes to tasting them with his mouth. *'Don't finish. Don't finish. Don't let this end. Dorabella, Dorabella, I want this to last forever.'* Dorabella and Spence moaned as they erupted together.

"Let's celebrate with something special." Dorabella walked over to the cabinet. She returned with two goblets filled with a green and blue beverage that emitted smoke. "Drink with me." She handed him a glass.

"Do I have a choice?"

Dorabella chuckled. She tapped his glass. Spence followed her lead and downed his drink in one gulp.

"Let me catch my breath. A breath of your lovely aroma, my Queen Dorabella." Spence kissed her lips. He lay on his back, letting thoughts of her carry him away.

Dorabella snapped her fingers. Wanda, Weena, and Lola entered the room. Before Spence's mind returned from his reverie, Lola mounted him. Spence drifted off into the euphoria of the moment. Lola moved like a piston while gripping his pectorals. He admired her red hair, scattering about like water from a lawn sprinkler. A tinge of guilt intruded. Spence looked to his right. His blurred vision saw Dorabella and Wanda pleasuring each other. A second later, Weena mounted his face and squeezed with her inner thighs. Her nectar tasted different from Dorabella's, but still ambrosial. A cacophony of female moans echoed from the walls…*Spence remembered waiting in the dressing room with the other wrestlers after performing before a full house at the Los Angeles Memorial Sports Arena. They waited for promoter Siman Beck, expecting a cash bonus for the successful show. Beck walked in with an attendant who rolled in a movie projector with 16-millimeter movie reel. "I have a bonus for you." The promoter showed the movie. "Enjoy boys. You earned it." It was hardcore pornography. Spence chuckled on recalling how he and the wrestlers found it amusing rather than arousing. They cheered the performers on and mocked their cheesy bedroom talk.* Spence turned and saw Dorabella, Wanda, and Lola pleasuring each other. "Welcome to Sonoria, Spence."

***

Spence and Dorabella lay on their sides, facing one another. They smiled and gently kissed. Spence stood and walked to the edge of the room. The sea had taken an emerald gleam.

Dorabella walked over and clutched his arm. "The sea has taken a new aspect. Is it pleasing to you?"

"Yes. Of course." Spence looked at the horizon.

"I sense something is wrong, my love. Did not Wanda, Weena, and Lola please you as they pleased me? They belong to both of us. Don't feel guilty. I am happy they made you happy."

Spence kept his gaze straight ahead. "It's not that."

"Did Wanda make you jealous? She belongs to you too. You may take her for your pleasure and at your calling." Dorabella smiled. "Better. Let's both pleasure her at once." She clutched Spence's shoulders and turned him toward her.

"You don't understand. We belong to each other out of love. We chose to love each other. Wanda, Weena, and Lola are like chattel. They had no choice. They did what they considered a duty."

"No, Spence," Dorabella placed her hands on his chest. "They love us. They love their king and queen."

"Either that or get tossed alive in the volcano." Spence backed away from Dorabella. "I told you before, in my world, slavery, any kind of slavery, is wrong and at every level."

"Weena, Wanda, and Lola do love us. We love them too, but not like we love each other. We are both comelier than any male or female minion. We also treat them better than they could ever expect from a minion man," Dorabella winked, "or woman. They live in our palace rather than thatched huts. They get to eat the bounty of the sea and other foods forbidden to the minions."

"They should be with their people. They should be wives and mothers."

"Are they not like our wives?"

"No. No. No," Spence squeezed his head. "The wine, the sex, everything about Sonoria, the whole thing feels like I'm on what the Beatniks call a trip. I know I shouldn't complain. Yet I'm looking for more than a childish masturbatory fantasy. I've only heard the overture in World War II movies. But my literature class taught us the story behind Wagner's *Tannhauser* and his stay in Venusberg. The endless hedonism of it all got to him. My Literature courses at UCLA also taught Homer's Odyssey and Keats's *La Belle Dame sans Merci*. They express the same theme. Those are fictional characters finding themselves in a make-believe land. As the saying goes, sometimes reality is stranger than fiction. Although the wine you have me drink blurs that line. Look Dorabella, I'm not a horny teenager or a dirty old man. I want true love with just you, and you alone." He pointed at her. "I want children and a family. Okay," Spence held up his hands. "I'm not a monk either. There are plenty of men who would consider my situation the ultimate fantasy. I know I once did. But I want more than an endless orgy with a bunch of sex slaves. I want you to be my wife and mother to my children."

"If Weena, Wanda, Lola, and I are not enough for you, remember, Sonoria plays by different rules than your world." Dorabella snapped her fingers. A tall, athletic young man with a handsome face and thick blond hair entered. He was naked and at full staff. "He can either join us, or you can have him alone. Either way, I will understand and be happy for you."

Spence looked him over and bit his lip. "No! No! I'm not queer! Tell your Johnny Bright to take a hike. Get this through your beautiful but thick skull: I love and want you and only you." He shook his hands. "I'll give you time to think about that. I'm leaving."

"No." Dorabella grabbed his arm. "You are forbidden to leave palace grounds without me."

"Says who? You can't keep me prisoner. I'm leaving."

"Jari Kavumba commands you to stay! Stop!" Dorabella now held Spence's arm with both hands and dropped to her knees. "You will anger him. He might make the Volcano erupt and destroy Sonoria in a river of fire and brimstone."

"I'm not religious, but I'll say it again." Spence pursed his lips. "My parents made me attend Sunday school. I was taught that Jesus loves us. I don't feel so much as a smidgeon of love from your Kavumba."

Dorabella gasped and turned pale. She released her grip on Spence's arm and put her hands over her chest.

Spence furrowed his brow. Don't worry, Dorabella. Your Kavumba won't destroy Sonoria." He opened his palms. "If he did, who would he have to boss around?" Spence jerked his arm away. "I told you, I'm not your damn prisoner and I'm especially not your slave. I'm out of here." He marched out of the room, through the palace, and out of the palace grounds.

Dorabella remained on her knees. "Come back, Spence! Come back! I love you!" She bawled. "I love you!" Her tears sprayed like a fountain. "It's deadly for you out there. Please! Come back to me! Come back!"

***

Spence marched over the palace's gold-tiled floor. He ignored the great hall's domed ceiling and frescos and bolted for the door. Once outside, he sprinted around the courtyard's pond and dancing fountain, stomped over a flower garden, and exited under the platinum archway. He did not return the palace guard's salute. He didn't feel the finely crushed seashells jammed between his toes. The mahogany and teak trees…the coconut and banana palms…all became a blur. He ran around the lagoon and climbed the mount adjacent to the waterfall. He stopped at the top. *'What a view!'* He breathed the waterfall mist and plumeria flower fragrance through his nose. *'I'm not winded in the least from my run and climb. Dorabella's latest elixir must be a powerful stimulant. I'd better be careful. I have no idea how it affects my health.'* "Who the hell are you kidding,

189

Spence?" He banged on his chest. "I feel like a million bucks!" *The lagoon. It looks so inviting. I wanna take a high dive.* Spence looked straight down and gasped. "My God!" He took a step back. "She looks even bigger from up here than up close." Carla, the great white shark, patrolled the lagoon. *'Rather not take a chance on that one.'* "Better move on." Spence found a path through the forest. He brushed aside bracken and frond as he ascended the volcano. *'What the hell is up with Dorabella? Thinking I might be queer? I made passionate love with her more intensely and frequently than humanly possible. What about me makes her think I might be queer?'* Spence laughed. "You're the one that's a bit queer, Queen Dorabella. Good one, Spence. Now you're married to a lesbo?" Spence stopped running and hit his forehead with the heel of his palm. *'Who the hell are you kidding? Her little show with Wanda turned me on. I'm madly in love with Dorabella. I know it, and she knows it. I can run from her, but not from myself.'* He again broke into a jog as he climbed the volcano. "I came here for Dorabella alone." *'Who the hell are you kidding, Spence? Weena, Wanda, and now Lola are gorgeous. I enjoyed every second of them.'* "Well, Spence, you got yourself into this jam. You dreamed of this. You went 12,000 miles out of your way to find it. You can't blame Nangolo. You can't blame Sonny. It wasn't too much drink or smoke. "You can only blame…" Spence tripped over a tree root tendril and fell face-first in the dirt. "Jesus Christ!" Spence climbed to his hands and knees. "Why curse him? I'm not even a Christian. Kavumba's in charge here. Why didn't I curse him?" *'Oh, well, screw you Kavumba, and screw your Sonoria.'* He extended his middle finger and brandished it at the volcano.

Spence climbed higher. The forest's flora transitioned from tropical to temperate. Greenbriar and sassafras replaced bracken and frond. *'These oak and chestnut trees. What happened to the teak and Mahogany?'* The foliage was no longer emerald. Deciduous fall colors of red, orange, gold, yellow, and brown ruled. Upon reaching a clearing, Spence stood on the peak of a ridge. *'What's gotten over me?'* He squeezed his head. *'Ever since I smoked that pipe with Nangolo. All the different weird, and wonderful wines Dorabella had me drink. Now I don't even know where I am. This valley. That mountain river. The fall colors. I swear I see railroad tracks on the far riverbank. Maybe I found a way out of Sonoria?'* "But where am I?"

Spence heard a rustling from the nearby thicket. He turned. Eight muscular men wearing war paint emerged. They pointed spears at him, glare flashing from the sharpened tips into his eyes.

Chapter 16

Sonny began his day at Koos Van Der Merve's Eetplek. Koos's radio played Jim Reeves' *"Distant Drums.'* "The usual. Explorer's Breakfast. Eggs over easy."

"I'll crack an extra egg if you'll make some of your luck rub off on me."

"I consider it blessed more than luck."

"That too."

"I never imagined this isolated little town, 12,000 miles away, would have . . ." Sonny noticed Koos wince. "I'm sorry. That didn't come out right. You've got better surfing than California, the best fishing on the planet, and amazing wildlife. So, finding the world's most beautiful woman in Henties Bay ain't a stretch."

"We're less isolated than you think. Alicia probably told you that we get surfers from Cape Town and Durban, sport fishermen from Europe, and people from all over the world visit to observe our wildlife. Alicia invites them all to her family's church." Koos laughed and pointed. "You're the first one to get past Leon."

"Remember yesterday when I asked for two aspirin to go with my Windhoek Lagers?" Sonny grinned. "Well, let's just say, I didn't exactly get past Leon."

"We've got to get you on a training diet if you're going to keep getting in scraps with much bigger men." Koos laughed and put an extra sausage on his plate. "Many locals have begged Alicia to represent us in the Miss South West Africa pageant. She brushes us off, saying she's too petite. I don't know about that. I suppose that sort of thing doesn't appeal to her. Besides, her inner beauty exceeds her outer beauty. I hope you appreciate that and will respect her accordingly."

"Of course."

"You better." Koos picked up a meat cleaver and grinned. "No, really." He put down the meat cleaver and chuckled. "The entire town loves her. They've seen you two together and they're talking about it. So, treat her right." Koos looked at the door and beamed. "And speaking of angels…"

Alicia entered wearing denim jeans and a cotton blouse. She wore her long, blonde tress in a ponytail topped by a sun visor. "That sure looks good," she pointed at Sonny's plate of food. "We have a big day ahead. I'd better also get some nourishment." She sat next to Sonny and nodded to Koos.

"Alicia!" Sonny beamed and kissed her cheek. 'She's so beautiful. Control, Sonny, control, this ain't the place to kiss her.' "I'm so happy to see you."

"You'll be even happier when you find out what I planned for us."

Sonny looked at her and beamed. Five minutes later, Koos put an 'Explorer's breakfast' in front of Alicia. She beamed, steepled her hands in prayer, and ate her breakfast.

"I don't know where you put all of that." Sonny said on watching Alicia finish her last of three boerewors. "But it sure looks good on you."

Alicia winked before eating a strip of bacon.

***

193

After eating, Alicia took Sonny by the hand and led him outside. Her Volkswagen Type 2 single-cab pickup truck idled on the curbside. Nangolo waited behind the wheel. Alicia had installed two rear-facing seats in the bed. "Don't worry. Nangolo hasn't smoked anything he shouldn't." Alicia laughed. "No one is a better wildlife spotter." Alicia faced Sonny, held both of his arms, and twinkled her eyes. "We're going on a wildlife safari."

Sonny returned her gaze. His mind went blank. He gave her a quick wet kiss. Alicia returned the affection.

***

"We've driven past here before, there's the Kuiseb River." Alicia pointed. "If we're lucky, Nangolo will spot a pod of hippos or bask of crocodiles."

"Sounds exciting." Sonny squeezed Alicia's hand. "If Nangolo finds them, please don't ask me to leave the truck."

"Are you kidding? After tussling with my brother, wrestling a crocodile should be like tossing around a plush toy."

Nangolo pointed at the river. "Over there."

"Look," Alicia also pointed. "Four hippos and five crocodiles."

Nangola drove closer.

"I don't think he should drive any closer." Sonny leaned in the opposite direction.

"Don't worry," Alicia laughed. "The Crocodiles aren't hungry, and they're nocturnal hunters. The hippos are another matter."

"What do you mean?"

"Hippos kill more people than crocodiles, lions, and leopards combined. They're fiercely territorial. If they don't want us here, they have their way of showing it."

"Let's get out of here."

"Relax." Alicia grinned. "Nangolo can sense they're not on edge."

"Why don't the crocodiles try to eat the hippos, or the hippos try to kill the crocodiles for invading their space?"

"They have an uneasy coexistence. Nile crocodiles are powerful and formidable predators, but the hippo has the upper hand. They are more powerful and aggressive. They can crush a crocodile with their jaws and tusks. Crocodiles may see a young, injured hippo as food. Yet a crocodile could never make a meal out of an adult hippo because of its size and thick skin. Moreover, they occupy separate ecological niches."

"As long as their niche isn't attacking this truck." Sonny breathed a sigh of relief. "I can't thank you enough for bringing me here. I've seen crocodiles and hippos in zoos. Yet I never had a beautiful African girl tell me about them while seeing them in the wild. This is a whole new ballgame."

"New ballgame?" Alicia laughed. "Next, I'll take you to a cricket match."

Nangolo suddenly floored the vehicle. Alicia and Sonny were almost dislodged from their seats.

"What's wrong?" Sonny held onto his seat's armrest. "Did Nangolo sense that the hippos didn't like us?"

"No. Silly." She touched his nose. "He can tell there's something else to show us farther upriver."

Nangolo drove for about three miles and stopped.

"Oh no, Alicia." Sonny shook his head. "Hippos and crocodiles are one thing." He pointed. "But rhinos are another. A rhino almost killed me and Spence on the way to Henties Bay. We barely escaped. "Let's not tempt fate twice."

"That must have been a black rhino." Alicia chuckled and held Sonny's hand. "These are white rhinos. They're far less aggressive."

"White rhino? Black rhino? They look alike to me. All have huge horns, and I'd rather not be on the receiving end."

They're almost the same color. People misinterpreted the Afrikaans word 'wyd,' which means wide, for the English word white. They're named for their wide mouths, not their color." Alicia smiled at Sonny. "I know. Afrikaans is my first language."

"I was hoping they'd be more dangerous." Sonny returned her smile. "Then I could kiss you goodbye."

"How about kissing me, Hello?" Sonny and Alicia kissed. Nangola looked ahead and smiled.

***

Nangolo drove them deeper into the bush. He stopped and pointed.

"Hey, look, Alicia! A pride of lions!" Sonny beamed. "It's what I wanted to see most. I wish they weren't sleeping. They look so lazy."

"They sleep up to twenty hours a day. Don't be fooled. They're resting up. Bringing down big game requires tremendous bursts of energy."

"I heard female lions do most of the hunting."

"That's true." Alicia put her hand on Sonny's leg and leaned toward the lions. "Nevertheless, male lions don't get a free ride. They must fight other lions and hyenas. They also chip in to bring down larger prey."

"Can Nangola honk the horn and wake them up for us?"

"Do you like getting startled out of a good nap?"

"Good point." Sonny laughed. "Rather let sleeping cats lie."

Nangolo drove for twenty minutes. Alicia tapped his shoulder and nodded. "We're stopping for lunch." She took a basket from the front seat. "I made sandwiches of sliced lamb and Gouda cheese." She handed one to Nangolo. "And just for us," she pulled out two wine glasses and handed one to Spence. "Neuras Shiraz wine. It's from the foothills of the Naukluft Mountains. Alicia filled their glasses. They gazed into each other's eyes and tapped glasses. She reached back and released her ponytail. Blond hair cascaded about while she shook her head. "It looks like we have company."

"Who? Where?" Sonny sipped his wine.

"Behind those bushes. Where Nangolo is pointing."

"I don't see anything."

Alicia laughed. "You don't see that elephant?" She pointed to the bushes.

"Huh!" Sonny put his hands over his chest. "How did he hide behind such low bushes?"

"You're in wild Africa," Alicia chuckled, "not at an American zoo."

"But he's enormous! And those tusks!" Shouldn't we get back in the truck?"

"I trust Nangolo. He has a sixth sense when it comes to wildlife. He would know if we were a threat to the elephant or if the elephant was a threat to us."

***

Nangolo parked the truck in front of the De Duine Hotel. Sonny and Alicia disembarked and faced each other. "The Land Rover isn't here. I'm getting more worried about Spence."

"Tomorrow, meet me at the church. We'll say a special prayer for him."

"Alicia, today went beyond special. I experienced something most Americans will only see in the movies. We saw lions, rhinos, crocodiles, hippos, and even an elephant. I would truly love to attend church with you tomorrow. I especially want to pray for Spence. I am afraid your church has something far more dangerous than a lion or crocodile." Spence winced.

"Don't you worry." Alicia laughed. "I have Leon under control." She put her arms around the back of his neck. "Not that I blame you." They kissed.

Sonny beamed. "I don't care if King Kong or Godzilla stands between us. I'll be there." He kissed her. "One more thing..." Sonny's throat clenched. "I..." He could only grunt.

"I'll see you tomorrow." She kissed him before boarding the truck. As Nangolo drove away, she turned and waved to him.

Sonny waved back.

Chapter 17

Delnoke emerged from the thicket. The warriors lowered their spears. "King Spence. The Guerlocks are poised to attack. As King of Sonoria, you command our warriors. You must return to the village. The minions and warriors are gathered. They are waiting for you to rally them for battle."

***

Spence walked next to Delnoke. The warriors positioned themselves to the front, rear, and flanks. 'I could stir up a wrestling crowd with the best of 'em. I could do it as a heel, Biff Rustler outlaw cowboy, and as a face, Spence the Golden surfer. Well, Spence, this isn't California. What do I say to Sonoria? Besides, I have no military leadership experience. I wish you were here, Sonny. Something from a bombastic opera might give me an answer. Think Spence. We're almost there. Got it! I don't know opera, but I did study literature. Orwell's 1984. Oceania is a dystopia. At first, I saw Sonoria as a utopia. Now I don't know what to think. Just think fast. I'm sure a little shove could turn Sonoria into Oceania. I remember Orwell's two-minute hates. Yes. That's it! After all, Newspeak lied. War is not peace. War is hate.'

***

All Sonoria gathered in the great assembly area. Male Warriors stood poised with spears, scythes, and tridents. Women, children, and the elderly stood behind them. Musicians and a female choir of a hundred voices sat in a gilded grandstand. Delnoke addressed them first. "People of Sonoria. Prepare to defend what is ours and what is sacred.

Fear not. For King Spence will lead us. Jari Kavumba has chosen him. He will not fail us!" Delnoke paused for effect before waving his arms. "Long live King Spence!" He nodded to Spence.

The Sonorians shouted, "Long live King Spence! Long live King Spence! Long live King Spence!"

Spence thrust his chest forward and shoulders back as he strolled to the podium. He faced the crowd with his right foot forward. "People of Sonoria. The Guerlocks are girded for battle. They are poised to defile and rob us of all we hold sacred. But you have nothing to fear but fear itself." Spence paused for the Sonorians to cheer. "Look around you. Count the blessings you enjoy, for the time has come to ask not what Sonoria can do for you, but what you can do for Sonoria."

The crowd cheered vigorously.

"Four score and seven millennia past, Jari Kavumba gave us a land and sea rich with bounty and comfort. Now we must sacrifice our comfort and embrace the hardship of war. If we don't, the Guerlocks will defile our land and steal our wealth. They will impale our babies on the tips of their spears and tridents, boil them alive, and eat them. They will kidnap our women, rape them, and force them to carry on their accursed race. They hate us, and they hate Jari Kavumba. The only way to defeat their hatred is to hate them more! Each day, let's take two minutes to channel our hatred and save our women, save our children, and save our land!

The Sonorians stood and cheered.

"When I say Guerlock, you say hate. Guerlock!"

"Hate!"

“Guerlock!”

“Hate!”

“Guerlock!”

“Hate!”

Spence pumped his fists. “Hate! Hate! Hate!”

The warriors brandished their weapons. The people shook their fists. They yelled, “Hate! Hate! Hate!”

“We shall reign victorious! Jari Kavumba is more than our father. He is our big brother! If he watches us, we win!” Spence paused for effect. “Big brother is watching you!” He pointed.

The Sonorians cheered.

Spence shook his fists, “Long live Big Brother! Long live Big Brother! Long Live Big Brother!”

The Sonorians responded. “Long live Big Brother! Long Live Big Brother! Long Live Big Brother!”

Spence turned and left the podium. Delnoke grabbed his arm. “Wonderful speech, King Spence. I wish to reward you with music. Queen Dorabella told me about two musicians from your world, Elvis Presley and Chuck Berry. Shall I lead our orchestra and play Elvis Presley and Chuck Berry songs on my six-string violetto?”

Um…Well…” Spence pursed his lips. “Elvis and Chuck Berry are unique to my world. We have the minions and warriors hyped up for war. Let’s not confuse them. As for your band, well, um, they don’t exactly play like the Tikiyaki Orchestra.”

“You earned a reward for your speech, King Spence. Moreover, the minions expect music.”

"Yes. You can reward me. Your female choir is outstanding. Have them sing for me. A cappella."

Delnoke nodded to the choir. They sang a vocalize.

'Oh my God. Their voices!' Spence stared at the choir. 'Their voices are ethereal! Heavenly! How can even Heavenly angels sing better?' Spence felt his brain tingle. He felt light enough to float skyward. 'Their harmony. Their melody.' Spence squeezed his head. 'Their voices are putting me in a trance. Each woo and ahh…They're taking me away. Where? I don't know. I don't care.' Spence's vision became blurry. 'The singers. So beautiful looking. Like Weena, Wanda, and Lola, Penny, Sammi Wray, and Alicia…Dorabella! Dorabella! Dorabella! You're more beautiful than them all combined. Each blissful note from your choir makes me want you more.' The choir effortlessly changed key. Their voices and songs became even more mysterious and enchanting. 'I love you more than ever, Dorabella! Where am I? Where are you?'

The choir reached a crescendo before drifting into a blissful silence. Spence saw the Sonorian minions drop to their knees and go prostrate. She emerged through a mist. His lips quivered. Her presence was the silence before the strings. Dorabella wore a pure white gown of gossamer-fine fabric. Its royal train extended for ten meters. Weena and Wanda held it up at the rear. Her burnished bronze skin seemed to glow beneath. She wore stark black spikes with gold bands around her feet. Her gown covered one of her diamond-shaped calves, thin knees, and lithe thighs while open to her other leg. A red band with an emerald-encrusted gold buckle swathed her waist. The gossamer fabric covered her breasts, nipples and areolas just enough to tantalize. A festoon necklace of princess-cut diamonds circumscribed her round neck. Gold and blue diamond earrings hung from her earlobes. The fronts of her hair were curled in wisps. The rest of her tress was straight and long enough to reach her heart-shaped buttocks. *'Her hair is no longer just golden blonde but tendrils of pure gold.'* Spence gazed into her copper-colored eyes. His knees wobbled and his jaw chattered as she approached. She put her arms around his neck. "I love you, Spence."

Spence imbibed her black orchid scent. "I love you, Dorabella. I am helpless in your presence. Yet you make me feel like a king."

"You are a king. You are King Spence of Sonoria. The minions adore you and have accepted you as their leader. Your speech was brilliant. I am proud to be your wife and your king."

"I don't need to drink it." Spence looked deeper into her eyes. "I want it anyway. I don't want it to end. I wish to drink more of the smoky, blue, and green wine with you."

"I will have Lola prepare it for us." Dorabella smiled. "Until then…" She kissed Spence full, wet, and long. The Sonorians cheered. Dorabella pulled her head back and winked. She led him away by the hand.

Delnoke addressed the Sonorians. "The party is over. We are at war with the Guerlocks. Warriors! Report to your stations. Minions stay in your homes. Arm yourselves!"

Chapter 18

The Appalachian mist shone with the light of dawn. After rising over the mountain crest, the sun gleamed off the grass. Penny Williams breathed through her nose and looked across the expanse of her grandparents' thoroughbred ranch. She deemed the barn, stables, paddocks, and half-mile-long dirt track secondary to her view of mountains, ridges, valleys, and the Greenbriar River. She strolled into the paddock and patted her favorite thoroughbred on the rump. "Good morning, Starfire. Ready for your morning workout?"

The horse nickered.

"Ahh…What a sweet thing to say. You know I'm happy to see you too." She stepped into the tack room and picked up a leather saddle from the saddle stand. She closed her eyes. The saddle became a surfboard. Spence stood before her, holding his surfboard. She imagined saying to him, *'I've missed you so much. You never call. Your number is disconnected. Where are you?'* The vision faded. Penny put the saddle on Starfire and secured the straps. "It's just you and me, friend." Penny mounted Starfire and walked to the dirt track. "Hojotoho Heiaha!" She yelled and nudged him with her heel. Penny stood in the stirrups as Starfire broke into a gallop. Smog-free Mountain air blew her long blond hair behind her like a streamer. Hooves beat a rhythm steady as a Joe Morello drum solo. They made the second turn. "Slow down." She pulled on his reins to steady his pace. After reaching the final turn, she yelled, "Heiaha!" Another heel nudge and Starfire galloped full tilt until crossing the finish line. "Woe." She slowed him to a trot. After about five minutes, she slowed him to a walk and rode to a paddock. She dismounted, held his reins, and walked him in circles. "That's a good boy. Tomorrow, we'll time you." She petted his cheek. "The Kentucky Derby is only ten months away. You're going to be famous. Will you still love me?"

Starfire nickered.

"Ah…I'll always love you too, Starfire." She pressed her cheek to his cheek. "Look who's here."

"Good morning, Miss Williams." The groom, a tall, lanky local teen, reported for work.

"Good morning, Harold. You know the procedure, please sponge down Starfire. Afterward, brush off the water and walk him until he's dry."

"Yes, Ma'am."

Penny walked back to the house. A car pulled into the driveway. She greeted the driver and spoke to him through the open window. "Glad you could make it. If we were back in California, you could blame traffic."

The driver disembarked. He stood nine inches shorter than Penny and thirty-five pounds lighter. "I got stuck at a rail crossing. The freight train stopped." He smiled with tight lips. "I had to wait until it started."

Penny chuckled. "Call the C and O Railroad and complain because I got to ride Starfire first."

"You're not the one who's getting to ride him in the Kentucky Derby." He laughed. "On that fine day, it's my turn to ride him. The railroad did us both a favor. Starfire got a workout with extra weight."

Penny tilted her head and half smiled.

"That didn't come out right." Vinnie grinned, "I'll let you have a turn with a short person quip."

"That's all right, Vinnie." Penny chuckled. "You know that I am grateful to have you on board. I saved Mountain Breeze, River Charm, and Blaze of Glory just for you." She nodded to the house's front door. "I know you came on an empty stomach. Mrs. Nash made you breakfast."

"You know how to torment me." He shook his head. "You know I must keep my weight steady. But I will settle for a cup of your grandmother's coffee."

"No milk or sugar."

"Of course."

"Go on in. She's waiting for you. Meanwhile, I have some errands to run in town."

***

Penny drove along curvy, tree-lined mountain roads until she reached the bucolic town of Alderson, West Virginia. The village was nestled in the Allegheny Mountains. The Greenbrier River and the flanking Chesapeake and Ohio Railroad bisect the town. Rustic businesses from the early twentieth century lined both riversides. Alderson's most prominent feature is a stone arch bridge that spans the river. Penny parked at Redd Nichol's General Store. She wore leather cowboy boots and denim jeans. The tails of her plaid, cotton blouse were tied behind her back. She wore her long, blond hair in a ponytail topped by a white Western hat.

"Good morning, Miss Williams. What can I do you for?" Redd Nichols was a gregarious, tall, and thin man in his sixties.

"You can do me better if you'd call me Penny." She chuckled.

"I don't know if a man over twice your age should call you Miss or your first name." He nodded in respect. "Penny, it is. After all, I always called your mother by her first name, and I still address your grandmother as Mabel. I sure remember your mother winning Miss West Virginia and almost Miss America. I didn't think this town could ever get anyone prettier. Well, one look at you and I know I thought wrong. Now you may have a horse win the Kentucky Derby. You'll make us all proud, although some folks here don't want us on the map."

Historic Camp Greenbrier for Boys sat across the street from Redd's store. A sign noting that the camp was established in 1898 marked the entrance. Two teenage counselors hid behind a shelf. They stared at Penny. "Uhh…Man…Dig that crazy chick." The boy pointed.

"You got that right." The other teen smirked. "She's a knockout on four-wheel drive."

Penny winced while trying to ignore them.

"Hey! You two. Get over here." A man wearing a white shirt with green letters spelling, "Camp Greenbrier Staff," over a picture of a green canoe with two crossed paddles pointed at the boys. The short, stout, athletic-looking man walked over to her, "My apologies, ma'am. I'm Lee Smoot. Camp Greenbrier director."

The two boys skulked over. Lee grabbed them by the trapezoids. "Apologize to this woman."

"I'm sorry, ma'am." The boys took turns speaking.

"You two lose your Redd's privileges for two days."

"No." Penny took her hat off. "Don't punish them on account of me. I accept their apologies."

"You heard her boys. She let you go this time. If there's a next time, it will be your last time. You'll lose your Redd's Privileges for the rest of the summer." Lee pointed across the street. "Now get back to camp."

"I'm Penny Williams." She extended her hand. "Gerald and Mabel Nash's granddaughter. They're teaching me how to run the ranch."

Lee shook Penny's hand. "Wow! Pleased to meet you. Everybody knows the Nash family. I heard you have a horse who may win the Kentucky Derby."

"Yes. My Starfire." Penny blushed. "I've seen your camp from the outside several times. It looks like a wonderful place."

"Yes, Penny, it is. It's my job to keep it that way. Moreover, our goal is to make good boys better."

"Based on how you handled those two," Penny chuckled, "I know you do just that." She smiled, "I know your camp doesn't have horseback riding. Call us at the ranch. Bring some of your boys. We'll teach them how to ride."

"Why, thank you." Lee smiled and nodded. "I may take you up on that."

Penny took a dozen eggs, a package of bacon, and a gallon of milk to the counter. Redd started punching their prices into his manual cash register. "I apologize for those boys as well. Usually, the Greenbrier boys are better behaved."

Penny blushed, "Boys will be boys." She chuckled, "My mother told me long ago that being pretty would have its downsides."

"Nobody would ever question that your mother knew what she was talking about." Redd tipped his sun visor. "Surely not I."

"And surely not me either." Penny looked at her watch in a fluid motion. "Hank's tack and feed should be open. Starfire earned a treat."

You have yourself a Good day, Miss Penny."

Penny chuckled, "Good day, to you too, Mr. Redd."

Chapter 19

Spence and Dorabella lay on top of satin sheets on a bed placed beneath an arched pergola of plumeria, hibiscus, gardenia, jasmine, and ginger lilies. Their bed was at the midpoint of a horseshoe of hills surrounding a calm bay. The geometric shape provided perfect acoustics for the Sonorian female choir.

"I know you miss your musicians, Elvis and Chuck Berry." Dorabella touched the tip of Spence's nose with her finger. "Is our choir not pleasing?"

"You don't understand, Chuck Berry and Elvis rock and roll…But…Oh my God…The female voices here… Heavenly…Their beauty…It's indescribable! Elvis and Chuck Berry make me want to dance. Your choir hypnotizes me with their sheer beauty! They're mesmerizing. They put me in a trance. Their singing makes me want to make love to you."

"What's stopping you?"

"Nothing could make me stop loving you, my Queen, Dorabella. This music, this wine," Spence sat up. "But I look at the hills. If they were blue rather than green, I can imagine we're at Dodger Stadium. And the bay," Spence pointed, "if the blue waters were land with green grass and a brown batter's box, pitcher's mound, and infield, it could be Dodger Stadium's baseball diamond. My Dorabella. How I miss baseball. I wish you knew just how much. If only I could help you understand its geometric perfection." Spence closed his eyes and looked upward. "The game is built on suspense. It has intricate plays and requires thinking ahead. Yet it erupts in explosive action. It's a team game, but it ultimately pits two men against each other, head-to-head, pitcher to batter."

"Sonoria's sport is 43-man Squamish. Rather than a diamond, we play it on a pentagonal field called a Flutney." Dorabella kissed Spence's nose. "It's a team sport involving almost all of Sonoria." She stroked his hair. "But you can teach them how to play your game of baseball with you."

"It's not just that, my queen." Spence gazed at the horizon. "I miss playing it, yes. Nevertheless, there's nothing quite like being in the ballpark with thousands of others to watch players of the highest caliber. The sound of the bat striking a pitched ball. The roar of the crowd. The banter of the peanut, hot dog, and beer vendors. Even the smell of the grass and dirt. But it's the players, Dorabella. The Dodgers have the best lefty-righty pitching tandem in baseball history. Sandy Koufax and Don Drysdale. Koufax. You must see him to believe his greatness. He has a blazing fastball, pinpoint control, and a devastating drop-down, 12-to-6 curveball. And he's smart. He has a deceptive delivery; the hitters never know what's coming. And Drysdale." Spence smiled and raised his hands. "He towers over the batters. He throws so fast that his pitches trail smoke. On top of that, he's mean and intimidating. If he thinks a batter is getting comfortable, down he goes! Drysdale won't hesitate to throw at him." Spence smiled wistfully. "A left-handed pitcher has an advantage over a left-handed batter and vice versa for a right-handed pitcher. Now you know why the Dodgers are headed for the World Series." Spence lowered his head. "And I hope you understand how sad I am to miss it."

Dorabella held Spence's arm. "If it's throwing you miss, we have competitions in throwing spears and tridents." She kissed his cheek. "As king, you can judge."

"Oh, no, Dorabella," Spence pulled his arm away. "It's like I told you. It's a one-on-one battle, pitcher against the batter. A pitcher can't be great unless he faces equally great hitters. The Dodgers will meet the Yankees in the World Series. They have a batter named Mickey Mantle." Spence beamed. "He has an unworldly fuse of speed and power. He also neutralizes the Dodgers' advantage. You see, Dorabella, he bats right-handed and left-handed, and he can hit 'em over 500 feet from either side. Koufax sometimes strikes him out but never fools him, and he's not afraid of Drysdale." Spence beamed. "Listen, Dorabella! The choir, the wind, and the sea…It sounds like crowds cheering."

"After battling the Guerlocks, we'll set up a baseball diamond. Maybe we can find a Sonorian who can play like your Mickey Mantle?"

"Dorabella," Spence rolled his eyes and sighed, "My world has over three billion people. Search the planet. You'll find Willie Mays. That's it for anyone close to Mantle. But Willie only bats right-handed. He hits homeruns as often as Mantle but not as far."

"Any woman who compares to me?"

"No, Dorabella! No!" He planted a wet kiss on her mouth.

Dorabella messaged his cheek. "Look. Weena is bringing us a plate of chilled oysters and scallops in their half-shells, along with Carabineros Prawns. Wanda is bringing us more wine."

"Oh, my Dorabella," Spence opened his palms, "Sonoria's wine would please the most fastidious connoisseur. But what I would give for a Lucky Lager! This must be the finest seafood on the planet." He held up a Carabineros Prawn. "Your seafood would be the envy of a billionaire on a luxury yacht. Nevertheless, just one, just one Boom Boom burger from Angela's drive-in." Spence smiled. "Picture it, Dorabella, three-quarter pounds of ground sirloin, bacon, onion rings, all topped with melted American cheese mixed with mushrooms. Yum Yum. Later, I'll take you to Juan's taco stand for beef tacos, pork burritos, or chicken enchiladas. Even a bucket of Kentucky Fried Chicken would do. We could go to a beach party with my surfer friends. I can grill steaks over an open flame or pork ribs swathed in barbeque sauce better than a gourmet chef. How does that sound, Dorabella?"

Dorabella blanched and covered her mouth. "Spence, Sonoria has no land mammals. It's only us and cetaceans. They are our forefathers and sacred to us. Our birds are only to beautify Sonoria. Killing one is a crime, Spence." Dorabella closed her eyes and lowered her head, "I'm sorry our food no longer whets your appetite."

Spence pulled the hem of her lacy attire aside. He imbibed the rose, jasmine, and sandalwood aroma of her cleavage. "Some things taste better than any food."

He helped Dorabella disrobe. While they made love, Weena, Wanda, and Lola fanned them with thick palm fronds.

A shrill horn blast interrupted them.

"Spence." Dorabella pushed him away. "That's our war call. The Guerlocks are about to attack. You are the supreme commander of our armed forces. You must report to them at once."

***

Sonny waited on the steps of the De Duine Hotel. He glanced down Jakkalsputz Drive. A beige Volkswagen Type 2 single-cab pickup truck sped down the road, kicking up pebbles and dust behind it. *'Screech.'* It stopped at the hotel. Alicia disembarked first. Nangolo and Leon followed. All three wore frowns. Their brows were furrowed and their foreheads creased.

"What's wrong?" Sonny ran to them.

"It's Spence." Alicia clutched his arm. "I have a strong premonition that he's in trouble. Nangolo got the same sensation. He even prayed with me in Jesus' name."

"What about him?" Sonny pointed at Leon. "Why is he here?"

"We need to look for Spence. Some Topnaar groups hate white people. Some of them consider Nangolo a collaborator." She looked at Leon. "If there's trouble, can you think of anyone else you'd rather have with you?"

"Good point."

"Let's stop talking. First, we go to the last place where we saw him." Alicia pulled Sonny's arm. "Let's go."

214

Chapter 20

Delnoke and two male assistants helped gird Spence for battle. His armament featured a breastplate of pure gold. His helmet was also pure gold, topped with an array of hyacinth, violet, and olive-green plumage. Delnoke handed him a shiny, razor-sharp sword with a gold, jewel-encrusted handle. His oval-shaped shield had diamonds, rubies, and emeralds along the edges. "Fear not, King Spence. They take orders from you. But you are no more than a figurehead. You can stand back and let Manubo lead the fighting. This will be what you call a naval battle. We will land on the Guerlock beachhead and fight them to a finish."

"A beachhead landing is more the style of the United States Marine Corps." Spence smiled." They're the greatest fighting force on Earth." He raised his thumb.

"Sonoria is not Earth. Yet I am sure your Sonorian warriors will not disappoint you.

***

Spence rode in one of four Korrak warships. Each Sonorian Korrak was twenty meters long and three meters wide. Each featured a figurehead on the bow. The Korrak transporting warriors armed with swords had a great white shark figurehead; the one with trident-armed warriors had an orca; and the vessel with the spear-wielding warriors had a sea hawk. They paddled ferociously toward an island. Spence's Korrak warship trailed them. Its figurehead was a carving of himself. Spence put his right leg on the planking and his left leg on a bench seat. He rested his right arm on his right leg and held his left arm against his abdomen.

The Korraks closed in and were now fifty meters from the Guerlock's island. "Hate! Hate! Hate!" yelled the Sonorian warriors. Smallish beings started throwing spears at them. The Sonorian warriors easily knocked them aside with their shields. The Korracks made a beach landing. Spence got his first look at the Guerlocks. Their bodies were dwarfish and somewhat pear-shaped. Their heads were misshaped and poorly formed, like a child's *Play-Doh* project. None had parallel-spaced eyes. Their noses were pendulous blobs. The Sonoran sword warriors engaged them first. They easily parried the Guerlock thrusts and lunges and slaughtered them. Some of the Guerlocks dropped to their knees and pleaded for mercy. The Sonorians beheaded them. Seconds later, they threw their heads into the sea. The Sonorian trident warriors impaled several Guerlocks, lifted them, and deposited their bleeding corpses into the sea. Blood steeped the sand. Guerlock screams of fear and agony resounded. Other Guerlocks fled. Sonorian warriors speared them in their backs. Spence keeled over and hurled. After gasping two deep breaths of air, he shouted, "Stop!" He jumped off his Korrack and ran onto the beach. "I command you to stop!"

Manubo scowled at Spence. Nonetheless, he raised his arms and signaled for the Sonorian warriors to halt their attack.

The surviving Gurlocks fell to their knees and whimpered.

"Look at them!" Spence yelled and pointed his sword at the Guerlocks. "They're retarded. They're incapable of fighting you. Do you see any Guerlock boats? How can they

216

be a threat to Sonoria? Manubo, return with your warriors to Sonoria, gather some food, and bring it to the Guerlocks as a peace offering. "You," Spence pointed at a Guerlock, "Take me to your leader. The time has come for a Sonorian-Guerlock peace treaty."

Chapter 21

"Look! Ahead!" Sonny pointed. "It's the Land Rover. Spence can't be far."

They drove to the Land Rover. Alisha looked at the ocean. The succession of crashing waves roared like angry lions while closing out at five meters high. She could see swirling currents and eddies interspacing the surf. A tear fell from her eye, followed by another, then another. She wiped them away and turned from Sonny, lest he see her cry.

"Alisha?" Sonny put his arm around her. "What is it?"

Alisha bawled.

Nangolo walked up to them. "I have heard the spirit of the sea. I have prayed to your Jesus," He pointed at Alisha. "Spence is in grave danger, but he's alive."

"You heard him!" Sonny quickly donned his wetsuit and grabbed his surfboard. "I'm going to find him!"

"No! No!" She grabbed his arm. "You can't!"

"Yes." He pulled away from her. "I must." Sonny ran into the sea with his surfboard and paddled out.

Leon put his arm around his wailing sister.

***

Making peace with the Guerlocks made Spence feel triumphant. He put his arm on his knee and thrust back his shoulders as he rode a Korrak back to Sonoria. Each of the warrior's oar strokes narrowed his thoughts to one thing. He closed his eyes, imbibed the sea's scent, and imagined the jasmine, rose, and sandalwood aroma of Dorabella's shiny bronze skin. A splash of seawater made him think of her minty breath and delightful nectar. Sunrays on the sea made him picture her golden blonde tresses flowing bounteously. He imagined the sound of the wind and water lapping against the Korrak as the Sonorian female choir sang to them. '*I miss so much about my world. Sonoria can never hope even to imitate it. But Dorabella and the heavenly harmony of the female choir surpass all earthly delights.*'

Upon his arrival in Sonoria, he beelined to his palace bedroom. Dorabella awaited. He stripped off his battle gear and opened his arms for his beloved.

Dorabella stood still. Her expression was hard and stern.

He stared into her copper eyes. They were bereft of kindness.

"What's wrong, my love?"

"When you first arrived, I couldn't wait for this moment to come- the moment that I say, 'Good riddance' to you." She pointed.

Spence blanched.

"Manubo's men are on their way. The ruling committee has ordered that you be thrown alive into the volcano as a traitor."

"What are you talking about?" His heart paused. He battled his urethra.

"You were foolish to show mercy to the Guerlocks."

"But, but," Spence's jaw chattered, "I acted on behalf of Sonoria. The Guerlocks are no threat to us. No reason existed to slaughter them."

"I have no say. Queen is an empty title. Delnoke is chairman of the Committee of Elders. They rule Sonoria.

They chose me as a figurehead Queen because my physical beauty and vitality surpassed all Sonorian women. Our race is dying. The Guerlocks are us. We are Sirens. What you were taught as mythology is reality. The Guerlocks are mutants born to Sonorian women and sired by Sonorian men. We exile the mutants to their island. We spread the propaganda that they grow into mighty beings bent on revenge against Sonoria. We control the minions by instilling fear in them. When the committee decides the time is right, we slaughter them as a ritual."

"A ritual to Jari Kuvumba? Isn't he enough to keep the minions in line?"

"We were once the handmaidens of the Goddess Persephone. Unfortunately, Hades abducted her. We were left to fend for ourselves. We invented Jari Kavumba to keep the minions under control. Your speech made a mighty contribution. The Committee of Elders has decided to replace the name Jari Kavumba with Big Brother." She paused, looking at the ground and shaking her head. "How ironic," Dorabella sniggered. "You made a groundbreaking achievement by establishing daily two-minute hates…Ha! Ha! Ha!" Dorabella's laugh was sinister. She prodded, looking back up. "Today, you are the object of the Minions' two-minute hate!"

"This is crazy." He hit his forehead with his palm. "You can't let Manubo's warriors kill me!" He shook his hands. "We belong together."

"Ha! Ha! Ha!" she prodded. "I never wanted to be with you. We hate humans. We developed our singing voices to lure any sailors daring to come near the portal to Sonoria into crashing against the rocks. To save our race, we used a mystical human who dabbles in forbidden arts to bring you here.”

“Nangolo? And why?”

“The Committee of Elders has ruled that we needed a healthy, strong, and handsome human to breed with me, Weena, Wanda, and Lola. It’s not what I wanted. I was raised to despise humans. Nevertheless, you were my duty to my people. You were easy to seduce and seduce again and again. It took longer than expected for you to take Weena, Wanda, and Lola, but you eventually enjoyed them too.”

“Oh, Lord Jesus.” Spence closed his eyes and lowered his head. “What have I done?”

“You must never say that name! The penalty for saying his name is death! Blasphemers are thrown into the volcano alive. You failed me, Spence.” She laughed maniacally. “And not just with the Guerlocks. We are more closely related to dolphins than humans. We now know that a human cannot bear children with a Siren.”

“I didn’t fail you, Dorabella. It’s biology that failed us.”

“Spence.” Dorabella started crying. “I am the biggest failure of all. I hated the mere idea of you. I only wanted to exploit you as my duty to Sonoria, and get pregnant with you as soon as possible, and then happily watch your execution by volcano. Spence. I don’t know what happened or how it happened. You made me realize I was what you called a slave, set aside as breeding stock. Males were kept from me lest I fall pregnant and give birth to a mutant. I was allowed female lovers before they chose you to breed with me, but I never loved any of them. I truly desired what I couldn’t have. A male body. Moreover, I never understood what you humans call love. I’ve lived my life surrounded by natural wonders, a perfect climate, and royal luxury. My title was Princess and later Queen. Yet I have known only emptiness, sorrow, and sadness. Only you treated me with dignity, value, and respect. I felt the passion of your love. I sensed you cared about me. Yet through it all, you stayed strong and noble. Spence… I love you.”

“I love you too, Dorabella. It’s crazy but despite everything you just told me, I still love you with all my heart and soul. Please.” Spence shook his hands. “Surely we can do something.”

“I wish I could join you in the volcano. I want the smoke from our burning bodies to combine forever.” Dorabella bawled. “The committee has chosen Manubo as my king. I am to bear his children. The Committee of Elders decided breeding with Sonoria’s strongest warrior is our best chance, now that humans have been ruled out. Spence, Manubo is rough and callous. He will treat me as his slave. He will only use and abuse me. He will treat Weena, Wanda, and Lola the same. When the mood was right, we enjoyed them together. Spence, before you, caring about them was my brittle thread to being a person rather than just Siren breeding stock. I wanted to share them with you out of love. Manubo will take them as his possessions and treat them cruelly. My life of emptiness, sadness, and sorrow now gets even worse. Rather I’d rather die with you, Spence.” Dorabella walked over to Spence and hugged him. They kissed. “I don’t want that to be our last kiss.” She led him by the hand to the water’s edge. “We have one chance and one chance only. A creature passed through the portal from your world to mine. She is my friend. Since she is not human or a siren, she might be able to take you back to your world.”

"Come with me, Dorabella. Come to my World. Drink a Lucky Lager beer with me. Eat a Boom Boom Burger with me. We'll go to the stadium together. We'll see Koufax and Drysdale; Mantle and Mays."

"Yes, Spence, take me with you. Weena, Wanda, and Lola can replenish our race." The volume and tremor of male voices and harsh footsteps increased each second. "Manubo and his men are in the palace. I can call her with my thoughts. Our only chance is that she is nearby." Dorabella pinched her eyes shut. She murmured an incoherent chant.

Spence saw a huge shadow approach the water's edge, right outside their bedroom. A dorsal fin, looking more like a mainsail, cleaved through the surface. He blanched and shivered.

"She's here. Fear not. It's our only chance. We'll jump in together. I'll ride on your back while you hold her dorsal fin. Breathe deeply. After you pass through the portal to your world, you will lose the ability to breathe underwater."

Spence hesitated. Carla, the great white shark, was even larger than he realized. Manubo and six armed warriors crashed into their bedroom. Spence grabbed Dorabella's hand and leapt into the water with her.

***

The storm surge paused.

Sonny paddled furiously to get through before the next set of breakers. Out of nowhere, a swell steepened to four meters. It crashed onto Sonny and held him underwater. Sonny spasmodically waved his arms. The turbulence shook him like a dog killing a rat. He saw only stinging, blurry saltwater.

'One chance. Do what the Hawaiian taught you.'

He let out a few cubic centimeters of precious breath. He followed its bubbles to the surface. Sonny broke the surface and gasped for breath. He looked up and saw another wave about to crash onto him. He did a deep dive. He stayed underwater until the turbulence passed. Three seconds after again breaking the surface, an eddy spun him.

'Don't panic. Don't panic.'

The whirlpool deposited Sonny in an outgoing current. It took him out to sea as fast as a drag racer burning up a quarter mile. He found himself offshore in the Benguela Current. The Cassimbo fog, formed by the cold water meeting the hot Namib Desert air, narrowed his vision to five meters.

Sonny felt too exhausted to tread water.

***

Sonny's surfboard had broken in half. Alisha spotted the pieces washing onto the shore. She covered her eyes and wailed. Leon put his arm around her. Nangolo prayed.

***

Dorabella clung onto Spence's back and helped him swim to Carla. The shark waited. Spence grabbed her dorsal fin. Carla took off like a nuclear submarine. Manubo's warriors threw spears at them. Their spears streaked through the water; Carla had gotten Spence and Dorabella out of range. At first, the speeding water blurred Spence's vision and stung his eyes. Dorabella, clinging to his back, was his sole comfort. Euphoria swept over him. The blinding water became golden rays. Soon, he saw a prism of colors. He felt like he was floating on air rather than cutting through water.

224

It ended in an instant. Spence had leapt into the water with Dorabella while naked. Now he wore his wetsuit and floated on his surfboard. "Dorabella? Dorabella! Dorabella!" He paddled his surfboard in a panic. "Dorabella! Dorabella!"

A cottony, white cloud appeared over the dishwater-gray fog. A woman in white stood on the cloud. She had wings of thick, shocking white plumage. He never imagined seeing anyone as beautiful as Dorabella. Yet this woman's eyes were bluer than the Sonorian sea and set a perfect eye width apart. Her indigo hair flowed to her waist. Her skin was whiter than sea foam while her cheeks radiated like jewels. Her lips had just the right thickness and were even.

***

Sonny performed a dead man's float, allowing his wetsuit to keep him from sinking into the abyss. He raised his head. He felt his heart drop into his stomach. A huge dorsal fin and caudal lobe thrashed only five meters away. *'Basking Shark. Please be a basking shark.'* Its tail stirred a tempest in the water. A huge, dark, shadowy creature rushed directly at him. It was no basking shark. The shark lifted Sonny from the water and tossed him. Sonny was too shocked to scream. The shark circled him, closing the gap with each orbit. "Lord Jesus, if this be your will that I die, please let the shark take all of me. Forgive me and take me home to you. But please spare Alisha from seeing my mangled body parts wash up on shore."

***

"I am Isolde Maria. I am an angel from Heaven."

"Did I die? Are you taking me to Heaven?"

"No, Spence." Isolde Maria chuckled. "You're very much alive."

225

"Dorabella! Dorabella! I want my Dorabella! Where is she?"

"I'm sorry, Spence. Dorabella couldn't pass through the portal. She is a being from another realm. You entered her forbidden world. Dorabella is not for you. She does not belong in this world."

"But I love her! Please, angel, bring her to me."

"No, Spence. That is impossible. I will comfort you with the knowledge that her pain and suffering are over. I know you love her, and you will mourn her. Time, knowledge, and understanding will heal your heart. Someday, you will have wonderful children with the woman who is meant for you. A woman you will love and who can love you in return as only a human being can love. When you get to shore, pray with Alisha. She will show you the way to saving faith."

"Where am I?"

"You are where you paddled out into the sea three days ago. Spence, a creature once from this world, returned through the portal with you. She is no threat to humans. Nevertheless, she is curious. Your friend Sonny needs you. Order the creature to the deep sea. Sonny is terrified." Isolde Maria vanished.

Spence started paddling. He spotted a man struggling to stay afloat. Paddling closer, he saw the huge dorsal and caudal fins.

"Carla! Return to the open ocean."

***

The shark flicked its tail and disappeared.

"Is it gone, or is she poised to attack from below? I must look like a seal in this wetsuit.' Sonny closed his eyes and prayed.

***

Spence focused on him. "Sonny? Sonny! Is that you!"

"Stay away. There's a huge great white shark over here."

"It's all right. She's gone. I'm coming over."

"Spence? My God! It's you! It's really you. You look awful." Sonny laughed. "But you couldn't possibly look better."

"Climb aboard, Sonny."

Sonny and Spence lay across the surfboard's width. "What time did you paddle out, Sonny?"

"Not long ago, in the morning."

The sun is breaking through the fog. It's in the West, so shore is that way." Spence pointed to the East. "Let's follow this Southerly wind and let it take us parallel to shore. I know there's a peninsula nearby. The closeout surf won't be so radical on the leeward side of the point."

"Where were you all this time? You look like you were stranded at sea."

"It's nothing, Sonny." Spence closed his eyes and pictured Dorabella. "It's nothing. I wanted to be alone, sort out my thoughts, and catch some waves."

"I saw what looked like gold dust by the Land Rover. Do you think there's any truth to the Golden Strand? Do you think the legend of Dorabella is real?"

Spence choked back tears on hearing her name. "No. She's a myth. The Golden Strand is a myth." Spence winced. "Just like the sirens- those beautiful women who used mesmerizing voices to lure sailors to their doom," Spence fought back a tear, "just a myth."

***

Nangola pointed southward. "They're over there. On the other side of the peninsula. Both Sonny and Spence."

Leon and Alisha looked into his eyes. "Let's go!" She jumped behind the wheel of their pickup truck. Leon and Nangolo followed. They sped down the beach. Three minutes later, they came up against a ridge that jutted into the Atlantic Ocean. Alisha spotted a clearing on the plateau behind the beach. She turned sharply and bashed through the brush. Several jolts and bumps later, Alisha made it to the other side of the peninsula. The sea was calmer on its leeward side.

"Stop!" Nangolo shook Alisha's shoulder. "Stop!" He pointed. "Look."

***

Spence and Sonny paddled and kicked their surfboard around the point. "Thank you, Lord Jesus. The sea is calmer here, and the fog is lifting. I hope Miss Great White Shark isn't following us."

"If she is, Sonny, she's only there to help us."

"I don't know what's worse." Sonny laughed. "Sharing the ocean with a huge shark or a surfboard with a madman. Help us? That shark could easily help herself to us as a between meal snack." He sniggered. "Spence! Look!"

***

228

"Look! Look!" Nangolo pointed to the ocean.

"It's Them!" Alisha beamed and jumped up and down. "It's them! Both Sonny and Spence."

***

"They're waiting for us! Come on, Spence. Let's catch a wave and get to them.

***

Like a scene from a classic Hollywood movie, Sonny and Alisha ran toward each other with open arms. They embraced and kissed.

Spence trudged toward Nangolo and Leon. "Water…I need water."

"Ak nee man. You look like you haven't drank water in days." Leon grabbed a five-liter container from the pickup truck and handed it to Spence.

Spence drank the contents in one gulp. After finishing, he dropped the container in the sand and staggered to Alisha and Sonny. "Sorry to interrupt you lovebirds. Alisha. An angel…um…I mean…Alisha…Can you pray with me? Show me the way to saving faith in Jesus?"

"Of course," Alisha took Spence's hand and led him away. They both dropped to one knee and prayed. Spence returned with a broad smile.

"You look hungry enough to eat a shark." Lean grinned. "I don't know what you and my sister prayed about, but God is good. He just answered a prayer you didn't even make. Today is potjiekoss day at Koos Van der Merve's. We'll let you eat it all."

229

“Lamb? Beef?” Spence beamed. “Yes. It’s great to be back.”

Nangolo and Spence made eye contact. They half-nodded with a conspiratorial grin.

Chapter 22

J.G. Strijdom Airport. Windhoek, South West Africa.

Spence stood at the departure gate. He faced Sonny, Alisha, Leon, Nangolo, and Koos Van der Merve.

Sonny walked up to Spence. "I guess this is it, buddy." They embraced.

"I'll see you later, alligator."

"After a while, crocodile."

"I wish you would come back for our wedding." Alisha took Sonny's arm.

"Me too." Sonny smiled. "And bring Rick and some wrestlers. When the minister asks if anyone has any objections to our marrying," Sonny poked Leon in the ribs. "I'm worried this big lug might change his mind."

Leon chuckled.

"We're going to stay in Henties Bay for the meantime." Alisha arched her eyes. "We may later move to Durban or Cape Town."

"Don't worry, Spence," Sonny put his arm around Alisha. "California is on the table. Right now, we're living life to the fullest in the present. We'll see where God takes us in the future."

"Well, Koos, I can't wait to devour a bacon and mushroom boom boom burger. But, damn," He pursed his lips and shook his head, "I'm gonna miss your potjiekoss, boerewores, and bobotie." Spence shook Koos's right hand with both of his hands.

Spence faced Nangolo. They made eye contact. Spence shook his hand, moved closer, and spoke without moving his lips. "You know my secret," Spence winked, "Keep it."

Nangolo smiled and winked back.

Spence took one last look at his friends. Tears fell from Sonny's left eye. Alisha cried openly. Koos, Nangolo, and Leon smiled and waved.

***

Spence leaned his forehead on the window. His South African Airlines flight to Johannesburg was ascending. It banked to the northwest. '*The Ocean…The beach…It's gold. No. No. It can't be. It isn't.*' He pinched his eyes shut. '*But it's the same color as her skin.*' The flight attendant walked past him. "Ma'am. Any chance you can bring me a moist towel? Please?"

"Sure." She walked to the galley and returned with a moist towel.

Spence put it over his eyes. 'Dorabella, Dorabella.'

A vision of the beautiful angel Isolde Maria intervened. '*You will mourn for her.*'

Spence pressed the moistened towel into his eyes.

Chapter 23

Spence and Rick sat on their Santa Monica Beach lifeguard stand.

"Well, buddy, I once imagined us working together as wrestlers. Yet here we are, teamed up as lifeguards. You breezed through the training: the rescue techniques, all the swimming tests, first aid, treatment of cuts and jellyfish stings, and CPR. You're the man."

"You're a true friend, Rick. Thank you for greasing the skids on getting me hired. Feldman and Beck ruined me in the entertainment industry. I sure can't complain about this, though."

"Have you heard from Sonny?"

"Not since he sent me a wedding picture."

"Yeah, you showed me. What a lovely bride!"

"Alisha. She's an amazing young lady."

Rick chuckled, "She must be if she can make an honest man out of a playboy like Sonny. I guess that's what finding God will get you."

"I found God after looking for the wrong thing."

"At least you can still drink a Lucky Lager with me."

"Jesus turned water into wine. Although I doubt it was like the stuff I drank over there."

"What do you mean, Spence?" Rick raised his hands and shrugged. "Yes, I heard South African wine is world-renowned."

"Never mind." Spence looked wistfully at the horizon.

"I hope you don't mind my asking, but what about Penny? Everybody misses her."

"I haven't heard from her since she left to stay at her grandparents' thoroughbred ranch in West Virginia."

"I'm glad you gave Feldman what he had coming to him."

"I lost my wrestling career over it, but it was worth it." Spence rested his chin on his palm. "If we did things legally, Feldman's lawyers would've gotten him off the hook, and it would've put Penny through the trauma again and again."

"You did right, Spence." Rick affectionately cuffed Spence's arm. "The incident must have deeply damaged her to cause her to leave California and not finish design school. I do hope she comes back, though."

"Me too." Spence looked at his waterproof watch. "Well, it's foot patrol time."

"You coming to the beach party tonight?"

"You really need me?" Spence climbed down from the lifeguard tower with his rescue can and swim fins.

"Need you?" Rick prodded and guffawed. "We never *needed* you. After all, Sonny was the life of the party, and Penny was the prettiest gal, but the show goes on. You can keep drifting in and out of the real world. Stop when you're in the real world, come to the party, and have some fun. Get over whatever happened in Africa and get yourself a new gal. You still look great, and," Rick guffawed, "you haven't completely lost your mind." He paused for effect. "Yet."

"I'll think about it." Spence chuckled. "If I can't make it, I'll see you here at five am for our two-man kayak row.

We're still on for the Pacific team versus the Atlantic team in Florida."

***

Spence conducted a foot patrol of the beach. 'All is in order. The Pacific Ocean is calm today. If the conditions were anything like a typical Atlantic Skeleton Coast day, I'd be pulling swimmers out of the ocean from dawn to dusk. It seems like forever ago that Sonny was besotted with Sammi Wray. I remember him telling me how every time he saw a pretty brunette, he thought she might be Sammi. At least, I'll never see anyone looking remotely like Dorabella. No tanned skin can match her genuine golden glow. No shade of hair is like her golden strands. I'll never again see copper eyes on a woman. A cat, yes.' Spence laughed at himself, 'Never a human.'

A young boy grabbed Spence's arm, breaking his reverie. "Hey, lifeguard. Didn't you used to be Spence Carter, the wrestler, you know, The Golden Surfer?"

"No, young man, I just the beach trashman. Don't litter and stay safe in the ocean."

An overweight woman in a blue, floral-patterned, one-piece bathing suit grabbed the boy. "Come along, David. He has lives to save."

"Aww…Mom," David pointed at Spence, "He's the Golden Surfer. I've watched him wrestle on TV."

"Leave the lifeguard alone." She yanked her son by the arm without looking at Spence. "And how many times do I have to tell you that wrestling is fake?"

***

235

Spence's shift had ended two hours ago. He remained seated on the lifeguard stand to watch the sunset, hoping to lose himself in his thoughts. *'The setting sun on the horizon shines like gold on the sea. I am lucky. Has any human ever seen the ocean sprinkled with real gold? Dorabella? Dorabella? Where are you? Are you back in Sonoria? Do you still exist? Did you ever exist? You were not human. You were a siren. The beautiful angel who spoke to me was as beautiful as you. She wasn't human either. She told me your pain is over. What did she mean? I hope she meant you're not back in Sonoria as Manubo's lover and slave. Must jealousy torment me too? Will I forever love you, Dorabella? How quickly I forgave your betrayal. Now I understand God's forgiveness. But what a price God the Father paid!'*

Spence spotted the distant glow of a bonfire. He reached into the lifeguard stand's equipment box and grabbed a pair of binoculars. He held them to his eyes and spotted a column of upright surfboards. People were dancing. Spence cupped his ears and heard the final notes of Chuck Berry's *'Johnny B. Goode.'* The next song was Elvis Presley's *'All Shook Up.'*

'I imagine Rick's having fun. I'm glad Jesus did the work on the cross, and I don't have to live my life as a penitent like Tannhäuser did. I remember my parents' favorite song, Vaughn Monroe's 'Beware My Heart.' I rarely listened to my parents' advice, and I especially never listened to their square music. Nonetheless, I should've paid attention to that song before looking for the Golden Strand, Sonoria, and especially Dorabella. Beware my heart. I should've listened. Well, let's see what songs are on the radio.' Spence turned on his Zenith Royal Radio 755. "Classical music." Spence looked upward. "Well, Sonny, if Nangolo is making it so you can see me now, you'll be proud. I won't turn the dial." The radio announcer broadcasted, "Our next piece is by French composer Claude Debussy…"

'Debussy? Sonny, I remember when we first met Nangolo, you spoke of a Debussy piece about the sea.'

"…and his three-movement tone poem, the Nocturnes. Movement one is the Nuages, it evokes an atmospheric tone of shifting sea cloudscapes. His second movement is the Fetes, a festival of the sea. The third movement features the California Women's choir singing the Sirenes. The Sirens, whose voices were so enchanting that they could lure sailors to their doom."

"Sirens!" Spence turned up the radio volume and stared at the starry horizon. After thirteen minutes of instrumental music, the women's choir sang the first note of the Sirenes. Their melodic and harmonious ahhs, woos, and oos transported Spence back into Dorabella's arms.

He cried aloud. "Dorabella! Dorabella! I miss you so much. I know what I feel. I love you! I don't care what you were. You were my wife, and I love you! I will love you forever. I know you are real. I know the Sirens are not just a myth. I miss you! I miss you so much." Spence cried his eyes out until the final note. "Stop it, Spence," he sniffled, "Stop it. Get a grip." He gritted his teeth and steepled his hands. "Lord Jesus, you're the source of all mercy, have mercy on my heart. Please stay in my heart. Forgive me and cleanse me of Dorabella and Sonoria. In the name of the Father and Holy Spirit. Amen. I'll see you in church this Sunday."

The radio played Beethoven's Seventh Symphony. He listened to it and admired the sunset.

Chapter 24

Dodger Stadium, October 6, 1963

'Sitting deep in the left field bleachers ain't like the tickets Sammi Wray gave Penny.' Spence sat at the edge of his seat, put his hand on his chin, and watched Sandy Koufax warm up to start the seventh inning in what Dodger fans hoped would be the final game of the 1963 World Series. *'But there's nowhere on Earth I'd rather be.'* He looked at the spectator seated to his left: an overweight, middle-aged man wearing a dirty white tank top shirt. *'But sitting next to Penny beats the hell out of sitting next to that dude. I hope he lights up another stogie. It smells better than his body odor, and he has more back hair than Grant "The Beast" Irons. Wrestling seems like forever ago. And Sammi Wray. You were classy and gorgeous. A little stuck-up,'* Spence chuckled to himself, *'but classy and gorgeous just the same. You caught Sonny hook, line, and sinker. You rejected him like a fisherman does a trash fish. I still can't believe he's married. Was it all months ago or decades ago?'* Spence cheered as Koufax got two strikes on Clete Boyer. *'Rick tells me they kept the scene of Penny dancing with Johnny Bright, and that Feldman is still in rehab. Serves the bastard right.'*

Spence looked at Dodger Stadium's five-tiered grandstand. The Dodger blue seats turned emerald green. The spectators' shirts became tropical flowers and plants. The green field turned sea blue. *'Dorabella, why can't you exit stage right from my heart? I wish you were here. Koufax is doing everything I told you he could. He's shutting the Yankees out. The Dodgers only have one run. That's all they need when Koufax is pitching. We're gonna win the World Series. No Spence, no. Never think about that place.'* Spence shook his head. He bought a hot dog from a vendor, held it to his nose, and let its steam seep into his nostrils before biting into it. "Yes!" He stood and cheered with the other spectators as Sandy Koufax induced Cletus Boyer into hitting a soft popout to the first baseman. *'Well, Dorabella, I wish you were here to see what's next. Mickey Mantle is batting.'*

The fan next to Spence nudged him. "That Mantle is tough. He's worked Koufax to a full count. If he can strike him out on this pitch, we've got the World Series in the bag." He lit up a cigar. "I bet Mantle can't even spell curve. Koufax will get him on a 12-6."

Spence shook his head. "You think Mantle can't hit a curveball? What else is in that cigar besides tobacco? Mandrax and Durban poison?"

"Huh?"

The next sound resembled a high-caliber rifle report, followed by a collective groan from the fans. Mantle hit Koufax's curveball at a launch angle of 30 degrees and an exit velocity of 155 mph. Spence stood and watched every second of it. It was headed toward him…It landed flush in his hands. It stung and vibrated; nevertheless, he caught it and held it to his eyes. "It's a whole new ballgame."

Chapter 25

New Smyrna Beach, Florida

Spence and Rick paddled a tandem kayak. They were beyond the breakers, rowing parallel to the shore. Rick glanced back. "Come on Spence. Put some elbow grease into it. The Pacific Lifeguards versus Atlantic Lifeguards events are just two days away. Come on! Let's go all out! We'll take it easy tomorrow and hope to hit our peaks on Saturday."

"Who keeps the trophy?"

Rick laughed, "You know it goes in the beach patrol headquarters trophy case."

"What do you say we keep pace with that jeep driving on the beach?"

"Great idea." Rick glanced back. "But you have to row in synch with me."

"Who's the galley slave here and who's the master?" Spence beamed. "Stroke! Stroke! Stroke!"

"What the hell am I going to do with him?" Rick muttered to himself. "Oh, Shit!" Rick stopped rowing and pointed. "We have company."

A massive shark, twice as long as their kayak, swam next to them.

"Spence, you say you learned how to pray…Pray!" Rick steepled his hands. "Please God…Please. I don't want to die."

The shark swam close enough to the kayak for Spence to look into its eye.

"Carla! You swam all those miles. How did you know I would be here?" Spence rested his paddle on his knees. "What do you want to tell me?"

Carla rolled her eyes backward into their sockets. A tough, fibrous layer covered them. Two seconds later, she rolled them back.

"Yes, Carla. I'll do that. Thank you. As much as I enjoy our reunion, you'd better return to the deep. By the smell of things, you're terrifying my friend."

Carla disappeared with a tail flick and a splash. Spence looked up and saw the angel Isolde Maria. She winked at him.

"Are we already dead? No way, I just saw you talk to the shark, and she obeyed." Rick was drenched in sweat and tears. "We'd better get to shore. I don't want to take a chance on her changing her mind. I'll sort out which one of us is crazy later."

"Rick, she's no threat to us. Let's finish our training."

"That's okay Spence. We've trained enough." Rick gasped for breath. "Besides, I need to clean out my swim trunks."

"That shark got me thinking," Spence laughed. "After the kayak races, I am taking a different flight than you. There's a place I need to go."

Chapter 26

Imeson Airport, Jacksonville, Florida

"Was it yesterday or forever ago that I was at an airport saying goodbye to Sonny?" Spence extended his hand to Rick at the departure gate. "Regardless of time passage, I will never figure out what's so good about goodbye."

"Are you sure about this?" Rick shook Spence's right hand and braced his arm with his left hand.

"When you look death in the eye, you tend to gain epiphanies. I know this is what I must do."

"Looked death in the eye? I call bull. You showed no fear of that shark. Maybe it was your way of keeping your pants dry." Rick picked up their trophy for winning the tandem kayak race. "The truth is that you didn't want to lug this thing back to California."

"Well, big lug, they're calling my flight. I may or may not return. But keep in touch."

"If you do return, you have your position with the Beach patrol waiting for you." He held up the trophy. "This should seal the deal. Make the right choice. You have a bright future with the beach patrol. 'Til then, you know I'll keep in touch, good buddy." Rick waved to Spence as he walked away to board his flight.

***

Spence gazed out of the Boeing 707 aircraft. It banked east over the Atlantic Ocean. 'You're huge, Carla. But I'm afraid not big enough for me to see you from here. Rick saw you, so I know you're real. But what if you weren't Carla? A friendly, great white shark who gives telepathic advice? Is that as unbelievable as making love to a Siren? What if Rick is right? What if I am insane? Oh, Lord,' Spence looked up. 'What if a wild shark was checking us out and was indecisive about biting our kayak in half and eating us as a between meal snack? Thank you, Isolde Maria. You confirmed that I'm doing the right thing. God is real and angels are real.' Spence closed his eyes, steepled his hands, and prayed. 'I hope soon it won't matter if the Sirens are real.' He drifted off to sleep.

***

Spence opened his window shade as the plane made its descent. 'There it is. I'm seeing it for real. It looks even better than in my old View-Master. There's the Washington Monument, the capital, and the White House.'

Spence had hailed a cab from Washington National Airport to Union Station. He admired its Beaux-Arts architecture before going inside. Once inside, he strolled across its marbled floors. Large arched windows let natural light shine on the gold-leafed accents on the coffered, barrel-vaulted ceiling. After transversing the Main Hall, he walked through a columned corridor, '*Here it is. Chesapeake and Ohio gate 25.*'

"All aboard." The conductor shouted.

"Wait for me!" Spence trotted to the train, climbed the boarding steps, and took his seat. After the train left the station, he admired at the Washington, D.C. landmarks one last time before crossing the Potomac River and reaching rural Virginia. After a couple of hours, the terrain soon became mountainous, replete with thick forests of trees boasting dazzling Fall foliage. '*Sure glad my window is on the better side.*' Spence admired the Greenbriar River and its wild rapids as the train entered the New River Gorge and Greenbriar Valley.

***

Spence disembarked the train. He gazed at the long, wooden station featuring board and batten walls, decorative brackets, and fancy stick work on the gabled ends of deep eaves. He read the location sign out loud. "Alderson." '*You arrived, Spence. You didn't quite find what you were looking for in Sonoria. Sonny found it in Henties Bay, South West Africa. Let's see if Alderson, West Virginia, can work the same magic for me.*' Spence walked inside and approached the station master. "Good afternoon, sir. Do you have a car ready for Spence Carter?"

The station master lowered his half-eye, wire spectacles on his long Roman nose, and read from a sheet of paper. "Spence Carter," His finger stopped on the bottom third of the form. "I'll call Lewisburg and tell them you're here. They usually take a couple of hours to deliver it. I'll treat you to a cup of coffee if you wait here. Otherwise, there's Clara Mae's café right over there." The station master pointed over Spence's shoulder. "If you didn't eat on the train, I suggest her Mountain Burger."

'Thank you, sir. That gives me enough time to check into my hotel and walk around town." Spence grinned. "And I may try that Mountain Burger."

"I'm happy to hear it." The station master tipped his visor. "Most folks not from these parts want everything right away."

Spence smiled and nodded before walking outside. He tapped his chest as he inhaled a breath of brisk, Fall, mountain air. He gazed across the clear Greenbriar River and

244

listened as it buffeted against rocks and rushed into rapids. He gazed wistfully at the surrounding mountains covered with Fall colors of red, brown, amber, and orange. Spence decided to stroll along the railroad tracks toward a level crossing. *'The Greenbriar River, that amazing stone arched bridge, and these classic American buildings…Wise decision to walk on the tracks. Linn Westcott himself couldn't design a better model railroad layout than Alderson.'* Spence followed the tracks for about half a mile, walking past the waterfront of Camp Greenbriar for Boys and Woofus Island.

"Toooooot! Whoooooo!"

Four Seconds after hearing the train whistle, he saw clouds of billowing black smoke from around a bend. Each second, a chuff-chuff sound got louder. He next heard a hiss and the ringing of bells. "All Right! That's no diesel." Spence stood beside the tracks as a 2-8-4 Kanawha steam locomotive pulling nearly a mile of coal cars passed him. "Here goes nothing." Spence ran beside the train, grabbed the ladder of a coal car, pulled himself onto it, and rode back to town. "Woo! West Virginia surfing!"

***

Spence walked across the stone-arched bridge. He looked down at the clear Greenbriar River. 'Damn! Look at the size of that bass. If Carla could make like a bull shark and swim up this river, that fish would provide her with a square meal.' After crossing the bridge, Spence walked on a sidewalk parallel to the river. 'Hmm…Redd Nichol's General Store. I could go for a Coke and a snack.'

***

Spence entered Redd Nichol's General Store, looked down, and perused some packaged cakes on a shelf. He grabbed a pack of chocolate cupcakes and walked toward the soda cooler. He stopped in his tracks. He never saw her wearing riding boots or a Western hat. There was no mistaking the identity of the tall, statuesque blonde.

She turned and looked at him. "Huh!" She gasped and clutched her chest. Her face froze. Two seconds later, the edges of her lips curled upwards. "Spence." She walked up to him and put her hands on his chest. Just as quickly, she retracted them.

"Penny. You look different, but better than ever."

"Spence. Where were you? You never called or wrote…Let's not talk in here. Pay Redd for your goodies and meet me outside."

***

"I should be angry at you for abandoning me," Penny blushed and lowered her head. "But I more or less ran away from you." She closed her eyes. "Feldman." She gritted her teeth and frowned. "You remember how I didn't want you to touch me after what happened. Yes. I know it would've gotten worse if you weren't there. Nevertheless, I kept how horrible it was to myself. He not only made me feel vile and filthy…" Penny closed her eyes and lowered her head. "You don't know everything. He sexually tortured me. The pain was unbearable. The evil in his eyes. I could even smell it in his disgusting breath." She raised her head and gazed into Spence's eyes. "I came here to recover and hope to find Penny Williams."

"Penny, you will never understand or believe all I experienced, or at least what I think I experienced. I finally learned what matters most."

"I told you that I loved you forever. I meant it. After all that happened, I still love you. I know that you didn't just happen to be in Alderson. I appreciate that you came a long way to find me." She pursed her lips and furrowed her brow. "It doesn't mean we will ever get together again." She stiffened her shoulders.

Spence blanched. "What do you mean, Penny? I still love you too."

"Stop." Penny held up her hand. "I'm different now. And I'm never going back to California. This is now my home. My horses are my love and my life. I had decided that no man would ever touch me again."

"I'm sorry, Penny. I should've stayed with you and helped you work through your trauma. I won't pressure you." He pinched his eyes shut and lowered his head. "I'll leave you alone if you choose. I am glad I made this trip, if only to say, 'I love you.' Spence raised his head and looked into her eyes.

Penny gazed into Spence's moist eyes. "Oh my God." She lurched forward and planted a wet kiss on his lips. She backed away. "I shouldn't have done that." She looked away. After turning back to him, she laughed. "I'll admit kissing you beats kissing a horse."

"Penny," Spence held both her hands and gently kissed her lips. "Penny, you're beautiful. I never said that often enough, I'm happy for the chance to say it now."

"Spence. I think you should go." She pursed her lips. "That's what I think. What I want," she beamed, "Is for you to stay. I'll let you decide. Firstly, forget about sleeping with me and then flying back to California. This is now my home. My horses are my life. Small-town life in Appalachia is not for everyone. There's no surf here, but we do have world-class rapids. We're not somewhere in Africa. Crosley Field in Cincinnati is just a three-hour drive away. You can even take the train. Pittsburgh is only four hours away, and Philly is only six hours away. If you don't mind the drive, you'll have plenty of chances to see the Dodgers. You can even play for Alderson's semi-pro team. Last summer they lost to Camp Greenbriar. They hate losing to the camp. So, I'm sure they'd appreciate your help. I'm not asking you to decide right now. Take a few days. Get to know the area and the culture. If it's not for you, I will understand. I will always love you, but I have a new life with the ranch and the horses." Penny winked. "The ranch, like the baseball team, could also use your help. I'll pay you with a Grandma Nash home-cooked dinner. I attend a lovely little country church. Join me on Sunday."

"Of course, Penny, I would like that. The past few months have opened my eyes. I told you I learned what matters most." Spence smiled, "What matters most is my love for Jesus. He has opened my heart to love you how you deserve to be loved."

Penny kissed Spence. She took his hand. "I sure remember Boom Boom Burgers from Angela's drive-in." She beamed. "A Mountain Burger at Clara Mae's tastes even better. Let's go."

Spence and Penny walked hand in hand toward town. "You never asked about Sonny. Believe it or not, he's married."

"Our Sonny? The life of the party Sonny? A new girl every night Sonny?" Penny turned to Spence and beamed.

"Yes. If you ever have the chance to meet his wife, you will understand why. She's made Sonny a new man."

"And you've already started making me a new woman."

Spence and Penny embraced and kissed.

A motorist drove by, honked his horn, and gave them a thumbs-up.

Epilogue

Fall, 1971

Spence and Penny rode their horses to their ranch's highest point. Six-year-old Allan Carter and four-year-old Alisha Carter rode beside them on ponies. All four dismounted their horses, linked hands, and shared the view. The Greenbriar River cut through the valley. The ridges and peaks were replete with Greenbriar, sassafras, oak, and chestnut trees boasting their Fall splendor.

"Look, Daddy!" Allan pointed to the far side of the river. "A train. It looks like one of my toy trains."

"Yes, Allan, it does look like it's from our layout." Spence then picked up his daughter, braced her on his arm, and kissed her cheek.

Penny pecked Spence's lips before hugging him and their children. "We're living the song, 'Almost Heaven.'"

The End